Critical Praise for Nina Revoyr

for *Lost Canyon*

- Finalist for the Southern California Independent Booksellers Association Award for Fiction
- One of the *San Francisco Chronicle*'s 100 Recommended Books of 2015

"Revoyr [is] an edgy and spellbinding writer with an uncanny gift for aligning human struggles with nature's glory and perils . . . With ravishing descriptions of the magnificent landscape, unrelenting suspense, incisive psychology, and shrewd perspectives on matters of race and gender, Revoyr has created a gripping tale of unintended adventure and profound transformation." —*Booklist* (starred review)

"[*Lost Canyon*] pulses with both beauty and terror, and the struggles of these characters, their physical and mental reckonings, are enough to make readers sweat without getting off the couch." —*Los Angeles Times*

"Linked to complicated national issues, imbued with layered representations of Angelenos, [Revoyr] has brought us an intellectually adroit, emotionally nerve-wracking, page-turning thriller."
—*Los Angeles Review of Books*

"What makes this latest from Revoyr more than a suspenseful tale of survival and personal growth is the slowly worked out differences of race and class, well articulated throughout . . . An absorbing read with good social context." —*Library Journal*

"This is an exciting, page-turning adventure story that reveals how good people can do things totally contrary to their own moral code, and the conclusion will both surprise and satisfy." —*Publishers Weekly*

for *Wingshooters*

- A *Booklist* Editors' Choice
- Finalist for the Southern California Independent Booksellers Association Award for Adult Fiction
- Winner of the Midwest Booksellers Choice Award
- Winner of the first annual Indie Booksellers Choice Award
- Selected for IndieBound's Indie Next List, "Great Reads from Booksellers You Trust"
- Featured in *O, The Oprah Magazine*'s Reading Room section as one of "10 Titles to Pick Up Now"

"Revoyr does a remarkable job of conveying [protagonist] Michelle's lost innocence and fear throughout this accomplished story of family and the dangers of complacency in the face of questionable justice."
—*Publishers Weekly* (starred review)

"Revoyr writes rhapsodically of . . . the natural world and charts, with rising intensity, her resilient narrator's painful awakening to human failings and senseless violence. In this shattering northern variation on *To Kill a Mockingbird*, Revoyr drives to the very heart of tragic ignorance, unreason, and savagery." —*Booklist* (starred review)

"Hauntingly provocative . . . an excellent choice for book discussion groups." —*Library Journal*

"Gripping and insightful." —*Kirkus Reviews*

"A searing, anguished novel . . . The narration and pace are expertly calibrated as it explores a topic one wishes still wasn't so current."
—*Los Angeles Times*

"I'll just say that this author is a big talent. Her book is a little thing of beauty. It's a story with American historical significance; it's a novel with emotional heft; it's a satisfying read in the spirit of what Picasso said about another writer, James Joyce: 'The incomprehensible that everyone can understand.'" —*Brooklyn Rail*

for *Southland*

- A *Los Angeles Times* Best Seller
- Winner: Lambda Literary Award
- One of *LAist*'s "20 Novels That Dared to Define a Different LA"
- Finalist: Edgar Award
- A Book Sense 76 Pick
- Selected for the *Los Angeles Times*' Best Books of 2003 list

"Fascinating and heartbreaking . . . an essential part of LA history."
—*LA Weekly*

"The plot line of *Southland* is the stuff of a James Ellroy or a Walter Mosley novel . . . But the climax fairly glows with the good-heartedness that Revoyr displays from the very first page." —*Los Angeles Times*

"Compelling . . . never lacking in vivid detail and authentic atmosphere, the novel cements Revoyr's reputation as one of the freshest young chroniclers of life in LA." —*Publishers Weekly*

"If Oprah still had her book club, this novel likely would be at the top of her list ... With prose that is beautiful, precise, but never pretentious ..."
—*Booklist* (starred review)

"An ambitious and absorbing book that works on many levels: as a social and political history of Los Angeles, as the story of a young woman discovering and coming to terms with her cultural heritage, as a multigenerational and multiracial family saga, and as a solid detective story."
—*Denver Post*

"Subtle, effective ... [with] a satisfyingly unpredictable climax."
—*Washington Post*

"Read this book and tell me you don't want to read more. I know I do."
—Dorothy Allison

"Dead-on descriptions of California both gritty and golden."
—*East Bay Express*

"A remarkable feat."
—Susan Straight

"*Southland* is a simmering stew of individual dreams, family struggles, cultural relations, social changes, and race relations. It is a compelling, challenging, and rewarding novel."
—*Chicago Free Press*

for *The Age of Dreaming*

- Finalist: *Los Angeles Times* Book Prize
- Top Five Books of 2008, *The Advocate*
- Best Books of 2008, *January Magazine*

"Rare indeed is a novel this deeply pleasurable and significant."
—*Booklist* (starred review)

"Reminiscent of Paul Auster's *The Book of Illusions* in its concoction of spurious Hollywood history and its star's filmography ... ingenuous ... hums with the excitement of Hollywood's pioneer era."
—*San Francisco Chronicle*

"Fast-moving, riveting, unpredictable, and profound; highly recommended."
—*Library Journal*

"Revoyr conveys in a lucid, precise and period appropriate prose ... a pulse-quickening, deliciously ironic serving of Hollywood noir."
—*Kirkus Reviews*

"It's an enormously satisfying novel."
—*Publishers Weekly*

"[Nina Revoyr is] an empathetic chronicler of the dispossessed outsider in LA."
　　　　　　　　　　　　　　　　　　　　　　—*Los Angeles Times*

"Quietly powerful ... the novel settles to a close as deftly and beautifully as a crane landing on quiet water."
　　　　　　　　　　　　　　　　　　　　　　—*LA Weekly*

"Revoyr resurrects the *old* old Hollywood, from the time before talkies, and dreams it into existence once again."
　　　　　　　　　　　　　　　　　　　　　　—*Bookforum*

"Nina Revoyr is fast becoming one of the city's finest chroniclers and mythmakers."
　　　　　　　　　　　　　　　　　　　　　　—*Los Angeles Magazine*

"Five stars."
　　　　　　　　　　　　　　　　　　　　　　—*Time Out Chicago*

for *The Necessary Hunger*

"*The Necessary Hunger* is the kind of irresistible read you start on the subway at six p.m. on the way home from work and keep plowing through until you've turned the last page ... It beats with the pulse of life ... American writers dealing with race relations tend to focus on black-white or Asian-white situations; Revoyr has the imagination to depict racial issues in which whites are not the reference point."
　　　　　　　　　　　　　　　　　　　　　　—*Time*

"Quietly intimate, vigorously honest, and uniquely American ... Tough and tender without a single false note."
　　　　　　　　　　　　　　　　　　　　　　—*Kirkus Reviews*

"Revoyr triumphs in blending many complex issues, including urban poverty and violence, adolescent sexuality, and the vitality of basketball, without losing sight of her characters. She creates a family, in all senses of the word, of characters who are complex, admirable, and aggravating; readers will root for them on and off the court."　　—*Detroit Free Press*

"Mesmerizing in evoking Nancy's love for basketball ... an artless soul-baring that grows deeply moving."
　　　　　　　　　　　　　　　　　　　　　　—*Chicago Tribune*

"A wholesome coming-of-age novel about two high school basketball stars, Revoyr's debut is a meditation on consuming passion and a reflection on lost opportunities ... Revoyr also evokes the feel of contemporary LA, capturing crackheads, gang-bangers, and car-jackings in sharp, street-smart dialogue."
　　　　　　　　　　　　　　　　　　　　　　—*Publishers Weekly*

"This book may in fact contain the most loving prose we'll see on basketball until John Edgar Wideman writes about his daughter Jamila."
　　　　　　　　　　　　　　　　　　　　　　—*Chicago Tribune*

A STUDENT OF HISTORY

A NOVEL
NINA REVOYR

BROOKLYN, NEW YORK, USA
BALLYDEHOB, CO. CORK, IRELAND

Published by Akashic Books
©2019 Nina Revoyr

Hardcover ISBN: 978-1-61775-663-4
Paperback ISBN: 978-1-61775-664-1
Library of Congress Control Number: 2018931227

Akashic Books
Brooklyn, New York, USA
Ballydehob, Co. Cork, Ireland
Twitter: @AkashicBooks
Facebook: AkashicBooks
E-mail: info@akashicbooks.com
Website: www.akashicbooks.com

For my father

"Biddy," said I, after binding her to secrecy,
"I want to be a gentleman."
—Great Expectations

CHAPTER ONE

It started for the same reason that so many other things did then, because of my need for money. I was a graduate student in history at USC, two years past my final seminar, lost somewhere in an unwieldy dissertation whose end was still nowhere in sight. I'd met my friend Janet at a café near campus—she was moving to San Francisco the next week with her architect girlfriend—worrying aloud, as I often did, about how to stretch my funds for the month.

Janet's hazel eyes lit up and she leaned across the table. "I have a job for you, if you want it," she said.

I paused for a moment before I answered. Theoretically, I had it good. Besides the $12,000 stipend I got from the university, I'd won a prestigious $10,000 fellowship from a foundation that supported research in American history. This had freed me from having to work as a teaching assistant, which was—although no one said so—the only money-making effort that was sanctioned by our advisors, who believed that anything besides teaching or scholarship was beneath our intellectual station. But the truth was, it was hard to live in Los Angeles on twenty-two grand a year—hard not only practically, but also emotionally, when guys I'd gone to college with were making huge salaries in law or finance; and the Westside was crawling with twenty-six-year-old tech millionaires; and the real estate boom had pushed prices to dizzying heights, making those who couldn't afford to go along for the ride feel worthless and embarrassed. My small apartment ran me $1,500 a month—a much harder nut to swallow after Chloe moved out—which left another three hundred and change for food, gas, car insurance, utilities, and anything else I needed to live. And unlike some of my classmates, I didn't have parents who could help.

"Well, what is it?" I asked finally, surprised by the eagerness I felt. It was like I'd suppressed pangs of hunger until an unexpected offer of food made me realize how ravenous I was. The day before, I'd spent two hours going through my old books, trying to figure out what I could get for them on Craigslist or eBay, and whether it would be enough to make up the money I needed for rent.

"It's *my* job," said Janet, grinning. "With the lady in Bel Air. She just asked me to help her find a replacement."

I vaguely remembered that Janet had done something, maybe secretarial, for some rich woman up in the hills. I hadn't paid attention because it was so far outside of my realm, and because Janet didn't really talk about her gig. She was in the history department too, but more cheerful and well-adjusted than any other graduate student I knew. Maybe that was why it wasn't surprising that she was leaving the USC orbit to complete her dissertation in a more glamorous locale. Her departure had been received with the mixture of wonder and envy that an escapee always elicits from those still trapped in the asylum. The fact that her dissertation—about some obscure counterrebellion movement during the French

Revolution—seemed to be going well just made the rest of us more jealous.

"Well, what do you do?" I asked. Then, remembering my manners: "Thanks for thinking of me."

"It's typing, mostly," Janet answered, but her tone was so enthusiastic that she might have said *swimming with dolphins*. "Mrs. W— kept journals for decades, and she hired me to transcribe them. Over a thousand pages, all handwritten. I just got to page two hundred a couple of weeks ago."

"W—," I repeated. The name sounded familiar. I realized that I'd seen it on a building on campus. It might also have been on a wing at the Natural History Museum.

"Yes, Marion W—," Janet said, sipping her coffee. "She's in her seventies now."

"Is it the same W— as the science building?"

Janet nodded. "Yup, same one. Her family was prominent in the early days of Los Angeles. Her grandfather came out to California in the late 1800s. He helped found a couple of the fancier suburbs, so she's actually one of the street people."

"The street people?" I said, picturing men in torn jackets on sidewalks during the Depression, holding tin cups out unsteadily to passersby.

"You know—Canfield, Whittier, Doheny, W—. The streets in Beverly Hills, which were named for the original families."

"Oh," I said, feeling utterly stupid. "How did you find her?"

"*She* found *me*. She asked the dean for a reference, and I guess he mentioned my name. She's really attached to USC—her family's had a seat on the board for three generations, and I have a feeling she still gives a lot of money. According to the dean, Mrs. W— wanted a history grad student specifically. She says we have a greater respect and understanding of how the world works than the flakes in the English department."

"Well, that's true," I agreed, trying to take this all in. A rich lady who'd kept a thousand-page journal by hand. This sounded about as exciting as watching a car get an oil change. Plus I didn't like the idea of what amounted to secretarial work. But the truth was I needed the money.

"You should totally do it, Rick," Janet said brightly. "The work is easy. Twenty-five dollars an hour, ten hours a week. It's not great, but it beats working in the dining hall, and the stories are kind of interesting. Only . . ." A shadow passed over her face, a single small cloud in her otherwise sunny demeanor.

"What?"

"Well, she's kind of *particular*. She keeps herself busy—she's involved with a couple of museums and hospitals, a fancy women's group. But she seems isolated just the same. Her husband died like forty years ago, and I'm not sure she sees her kids much. She's a strong personality, and yet there's something nice there too. I don't know. All that time alone . . . it's not good for anyone, you know?"

I nodded absently, not really paying attention. In my mind, I was doing calculations. Twenty-five dollars times ten hours was two hundred and fifty a week, or another thousand a month. If I started next week, I could make my rent this month. And the work itself did sound easy—I was a fast typist, could read all kinds of writing from the work I'd done for my father's business in high school. Sure, this woman's life was totally foreign to me, but that might make it interesting. Maybe I'd learn something about LA history—I was, after all, an historian—although stupidly, with what I realize now was the particular arrogance of the overeducated and underemployed, I didn't believe that there was anything the wealthy could teach me. This easy dismissal, this lack of openness to nuance and possibility, might have had something to do with why I wasn't a better scholar. It definitely had something to do with my failure to hear the hitch in Janet's voice, the warning about Mrs. W— being *particular*. Given Janet's general optimism, I should have taken notice of her sudden concern. But I didn't; all I thought about was my own burden being lifted.

The next morning, when I called the number that Janet had given me, I was surprised by the voice on the other end.

"2732," a young woman said cheerily, as if she were operating an old-time switchboard.

"Uh, could I speak to Mrs. W—, please?"

"Who is this?"

"This is . . . She doesn't know me. This is Rick Nagano. I got her name and number from—"

"Oh, yes!" she broke in. "You're Miss Janet's friend! Mrs. W— is expecting you. Please come at two o'clock."

It took me a moment to answer. "Two o'clock—today?"

"Yes, she's anxious to get back to work; she's been upset because Miss Janet is leaving." The voice had a hint of an accent. Was this a maid? A personal assistant? If so, then why did Mrs. W— need me?

"But I was thinking . . . I wasn't expecting . . . today, I have to . . ."

"Do you have the address?" she pressed on cheerfully, as if I hadn't spoken.

"No, Janet . . . Miss Janet said that—"

"Okay, well here it is." She recited a house address and a woman's first name. She gave detailed directions to help me navigate the winding Bel Air streets. "When you get to Jessica Street," she said, "you'll see a big gate with a W on it. Press the buzzer and we'll open the gate. Once you drive through, there will be houses on either side. They all belong to Mrs. W—." She paused to make sure I got it. "Just keep going on the same road until it winds to the top of the hill. The big house set back with nothing around it, that's where Mrs. W— lives."

"And will you be there?" I asked, still not knowing who *you* was, just latching on to what seemed like a friendly presence.

"I'll be there at some point. I'm Lourdes, by the way. I'll help you fill out the necessary paperwork."

I wondered, but didn't ask, what the paperwork was. "How will I know I've found the right place?" I asked.

Lourdes laughed brightly. "Oh, you'll know."

At twelve forty-five I left my apartment and drove to Bel Air. It was a gorgeous January day—the sky was clear and blue, the temperature was in the sixties, the warmth undercut by a slight delicious chill, the heart of LA winter. I'd had to rearrange my schedule—I was supposed to have lunch with another grad student to mark the start of the new semester, and then meet with my advisor, Professor Rose. Theoretically, I had planned to give my advisor the next draft chapter of my dissertation, but in reality I had nothing new, not a single line worth showing. In two years I'd produced about forty usable pages— two chapters—but then had lost my way. I'd like to claim that this slowdown had something to do with my other loss of that time, but the truth was that Chloe had left me in the middle of this dry spell and couldn't be blamed for it. My problem wasn't writer's block, which implies that something's there that just needs to be released. It was simpler than that. I had nothing to say. Nothing new or important, anyway, because there certainly was something *there*, maybe not ideas or content or logical thought, but the specter of the project itself, which lay frustratingly out of reach during the day when I sat at my desk and tried to grasp it, but awoke at night and seemed to fly all around me, as mysterious and elusive and vaguely threatening as a group of circling bats.

When I had my infrequent but uncomfortable meetings with Professor Rose, I felt the weight of her disappointment. She was the best-known scholar in the history department—the preeminent historian of twentieth-century California, author of several books that had achieved a measure of popular success, and frequent guest on the cable news channels when they needed an expert to place a current incident in a larger historical context. Getting her to chair my committee had been somewhat of a coup, a cause for envy among the other grad students. But when month after month passed and the seeming brilliance of my initial research ideas fizzled into nothing, I could feel that I'd become a burden to her. That morning, when I called and pleaded a family emergency, she didn't sound disappointed. She seemed a bit relieved, and so was I.

I headed north on Fairfax to Sunset, and then drove west on that winding boulevard through the clubs and restaurants of West Hollywood, the eight-story-tall advertisements on the sides of hotels, past the palm tree–lined streets of Beverly Hills. At the appointed intersection, I turned right into the mouth of a canyon. Immediately I was enveloped in green—the bushes and trees here were so abundant and full that it was as if I'd driven into a forest. The temperature dropped five degrees. The properties close to Sunset were bigger than any I'd ever stepped foot in, but as I wound my way through the narrow canyon and up into the hills, they got even more ornate, so that at some point they stopped being houses—at least by any definition I understood— and instead became estates. The walls of vegetation hid some of the homes entirely, but others were on display, built imposingly on overlooks, including one that had, in its own designated space, a futuristic-looking silver helicopter. I passed over the first set of hills and found even more behind them, a wide, complex range with little valleys and peaks, much of it undeveloped. I'd had no idea, looking at them from their base, that the Hollywood Hills were so vast. My only real experience of them had been the hike up Runyon Canyon, two miles up on the front part of the range. But farther back in the hills was an entirely different world, a private, lush, green LA hidden from the rest of the city. At the designated street, I turned left, and now I could see the ocean. The winding road grew narrower and seemed to go on forever, and I was just starting to think that I might have gone too far when I saw the gate that Lourdes had mentioned. This was definitely no regular iron gate. It was made of some expensive metal—could it really be gold?—and anchored in heavy stone pillars on either side, which in turn were encased in ten-foot walls. There was a W in curling cursive on the front of the gate. To the left, a small box with a speaker and number pad. I punched the button, heard a buzz, and the gate drew open.

Within the gate I saw more houses, set farther apart along the rolling hillside. But it felt different now, like I'd driven into a new country. All the way up the canyon, the hills had been green from the winter rains, but inside the gates, everything was even brighter, cleaner, as if the ever-present filter of LA smog was not permitted on the premises. The most colorful flowers I'd ever seen—orange, purple, yellow, red—lined the road on both sides. Here were two waving men on bicycles—residents? employees?—and then huge trees overhanging either side of the road. A peacock strutted out in front of me and spread his glorious tail; then he drew himself in and continued on his way. There were other animals grazing in the distance—llamas? goats?—as well as a rabbit that scurried alarmingly right in front of my car. The road narrowed and the trees drew closer together, and then finally I was in the open again. In front of me now, set off by itself on a little rise, stood the biggest house I'd ever laid eyes on.

In articles about the W— family, and in Mrs. W—'s own journals, the house—formally known as Casa del Cielo—is described as a mansion. In my mind, it was more like a castle. Built of white stones that had been imported from Italy, layered with turrets and parapets that might have hidden armed sentinels, it looked impenetrable, unapproachable; I half-expected it to be surrounded by a moat. The gardens—which even in mid-January appeared to be in full bloom—were expansive and lush, and reminded me of the Huntington Gardens in Pasadena; later I'd learn they'd been designed by the same man. In the open garage, itself bigger than most houses, I spied two large, expensive-looking cars—a Bentley, I learned later, and a Rolls Royce. To the right of the house, there was a dark-blue pool that was fed by a stone fountain with an angel atop it. Water poured from the angel's mouth, and the angel itself, in her muteness, looked at me with bright, desperate eyes.

For perhaps the first time, taking in all of this splendor, I felt self-conscious about my appearance. I was dressed in the nicest of my casual clothes—khakis ironed to the best of my limited ability, a blue button-down shirt from the Gap, and brown loafers I hadn't taken the trouble to shine. At USC, I'd never thought about my clothes. Sure, there were a few rich kids who wore expensive threads (it was, after all, the University of Spoiled Children), but they were outnumbered by students trying to stretch every dollar, and there was a certain cache to grad student poverty, casual outfits put together from items scavenged from secondhand shops, mixed with a few new things from the Gap or J.Crew. But suddenly, my clothes seemed completely inelegant, as did my car, a ten-year-old Honda passed down from my family.

But there was nothing I could do about this now, so I took a deep breath and got out of the car. I approached the front door determined to knock with as much confidence as I could muster, but when I reached the steps,

I noticed that the door—made of honey-colored, heavy, ornately carved wood—was ajar. "Hello?" I called out tentatively, and my voice echoed through what I could see from the stoop was a cavernous front hall. "Hello!" I said again, more loudly, when there'd been no response. This time, an answer, a woman's voice, different from the one I'd heard on the phone that morning.

"The door is open, young man. Come in."

I pushed the door open, stepped into the front hall-way, and stood there, not sure what to do. Everything in the entrance hall—including the floor—appeared to be made of marble. The space was huge—bigger not only than my apartment, but probably also the house I'd grown up in. Doors on either side led to what looked like sitting rooms, and a long, winding staircase hugged the wall to the right. Other than a large chandelier, I didn't see any lights, and yet the entire space was suf-fused with brightness because of the broad rectangu-lar windows near the top of the double-high ceilings. There was hardly any furniture except a tall side table that might have held mail or keys, and a hard-backed chair against the wall halfway down on the right, placed as if for visitors who needed a breath as they made their way across the large room. The only piece of art was a colorful painting, maybe eight feet across, that hung on the wall to the left. It depicted a garden maze, a series of rectangular bushes, with a cheerful, bright town visible in the distance. A boy was walking through the maze, still close to the outer edges; near the center was a girl in a bright red dress, looking the other direction.

I must have stood there for two or three minutes, but there was no further greeting. This was very strange—no

Lourdes, no butler, no person of any kind. I had a feeling
that Mrs. W— was hidden somewhere, watching—a feeling that turned out to be true. My eyes followed the staircase; I expected her to descend dramatically like some
movie star of old, but this was not—I learned quickly—
her style. When the voice came again, it startled me so
much that I jumped. She'd come in silently through a
door on the left.

"A magnificent house, is it not?"

I turned to the source of the voice, a slender, silver-
haired woman standing fifteen feet away. It took me
a moment to gather my wits. "Yes ma'am," I finally
managed.

"My grandfather had it built in the 1940s. We used
to own this entire hill."

My heart was racing as I considered the woman in
front of me. Janet had said she was in her midseventies,
but she looked like no other seventy-something woman
I'd ever seen. She stood about 5'4"—six inches shorter
than me—and had perfect posture, as erect as a young
girl who'd just left her manners lessons. Her shoulder-
length silver hair was combed back perfectly off of her
face, the edges slightly curled. There were wrinkles at
her eyes and mouth, but also a tremendous liveliness
to her face and expression. Her clothes—gray slacks,
white blouse, and a long blue sweater with gray ac-
cents—were expensive-looking and elegant. The diamond earrings she wore were probably worth more
than I lived on in a year. As she gestured with her
hands to speak of the house, I saw the fineness of her
bones. I had never known a woman of this age could
be so beautiful.

"It looks . . ." I began, not knowing the proper thing to say. "It looks like you still own a lot of it."

She turned toward me now, her eyes passing over my face, my body, my clothes. I felt as exposed and scrutinized as I did when I stood naked at the doctor's. "You're a friend of Janet's?" she asked.

"Yes, we're in graduate school together," I replied, glad for a question I could answer.

"You're not her boyfriend, are you?"

"N-no," I said. Apparently the conversations between Janet and Mrs. W— had not been very personal. "She and I are just friends."

"That's good. You're too handsome for her. And she's probably too much of a handful for you. You look like an earnest young man."

I didn't know how to reply to this, so I awkwardly shrugged my shoulders.

Mrs. W— didn't seem to notice. "Janet's a smart girl," she continued. "She surpassed my expectations. But she told me that she thinks you're even smarter."

I blushed. Janet couldn't have meant this; she was the one who was almost done with her dissertation! Maybe she was just trying to put Mrs. W— at ease. "I don't know about that," I said.

"What is your name again?"

"Rick."

"Rick what?"

"Nagano."

"Nagano," she repeated. "Japanese?"

"Yes."

"Well, that's all right," she said. Then, looking at me more closely: "Funny, you don't look Japanese."

"My father's Japanese," I said, launching into the familiar explanation. "And my mother's Polish."

"I wouldn't have been able to tell." I was never sure what people expected me to say to this. *Thank you? Really? What exactly did you think?* But Mrs. W— considered me more closely, and surprised me. "Yes, I would have. I know quite a few mixed-race Japanese, actually. I spent a lot of time in Japan. The bustle and energy of Tokyo are interesting, but I prefer the history and culture of Kyoto. The art there, and the buildings, have been very well preserved. Of course, the countryside is beautiful too. Especially Nagano Prefecture, where your people are probably from."

Actually, my family roots were in Okayama Prefecture—not that I'd know the difference. "I've never been," I said.

"Never? How old are you?"

"Thirty-two."

"Thirty-two," she said. "And still a student."

I tried not to feel defensive, but I couldn't help myself. There were plenty of grad students over thirty, I wanted to say. And some who were even further behind than me.

"Married?" Mrs. W— asked me now.

"Excuse me?"

"Are you married?"

"Um, no."

"Well. That's good. People shouldn't tie themselves up too young. Married is married forever."

I didn't point out that she thought me too young for marriage after suggesting I was lagging in other areas. Either way, I didn't want to talk about my own romantic affairs. Instead, I just stood silently until my new employer said, "Well, come on then. Let's get you to work."

With that, she turned and led me through the door at the back of the entrance hall, which opened into a large, dark room. It was filled with a mishmash of heavy furniture, antiques that looked more suitable for display than for use. On the tables and walls were various pieces, presumably from Asia and Africa—porcelain and ivory carvings, block-print paintings, a mournful oblong mask. A huge wardrobe of sorts—or something like it—stood in one corner, an ominous presence looming over the rest of the room. There seemed to be no design or theme to the room, other than as a receptacle for someone's expensive souvenirs from their far-ranging, adventurous travels.

And in a way I was right, for when Mrs. W— saw me looking, she said, "Useless, isn't it? All of it. These are from my grandfather's trips abroad. I never even sit in this room."

"It's all beautiful," I said.

"It is not. *Some* of it is. That bureau over there—" she pointed to a massive wooden piece, as big as a mantle in a hunting lodge, with carved heads of hawks and wolves, "that bureau is from England, the mid-1600s. That mask is from Nigeria, 1872. And *that*—" she pointed toward a strange upholstered piece, which looked like a chair bent backward, its arms pointed up in the air, "that's a *siège d'amour*, from France, the 1700s. So heavy men—like Prince Edward VIII—could make love without crushing their lovers."

Now I noticed the two sets of gold or brass stirrups,

one for the person lying back, one, presumably, for the person bending over. I must have laughed in surprise, because Mrs. W— chuckled. "Oh, so you *do* have a sense of humor. That's good. I was starting to worry."

From there we passed into a kind of open through-way, with a sliding glass door that led to a garden. At the door, two Lhasa apsos were barking to be let inside.

"That's Pinot and Chardonnay," she said. "They're ten years old and a pain in my behind. Hello, you little monsters!" she called out in a singsongy voice. "I'll be right there! Hold your horses!"

"Pinot grigio or pinot noir?" I asked.

"Pinot noir. We *are* in California."

"They're cute," I said, although I wasn't fond of small dogs.

"They're all right for lap dogs," Mrs. W— said, as if she'd read my mind. "I prefer sporting dogs myself. My father used to breed Brittany spaniels, and we'd take them up north to hunt pheasants and grouse. I loved those dogs, but they need so much exercise. They wouldn't be practical for me anymore."

"You hunted?"

"Yes, I was a very good shot!" she said, as if offended I hadn't known. "I was better than the boys my age, which was sometimes a problem. Men don't like to be bettered by women." She looked back at me, and turned into a hallway, where we passed what appeared to be another living room, and then another. "I rode horses too, competitively, but also sometimes to help my father out on his ranch in Santa Barbara. I wasn't one of those useless rich girls, you see, staying at home with my dolls. I liked to be outdoors *doing* things. And I spent as much time as

I could with my father. I was the apple of his eye, you see. Everybody said so." ¨

"I'm sure you were." I would have liked to say that I was the apple of my father's eye too, and I had been once. My father was an electrician, as his father had been before him. I was "the smart one," the son who got a scholarship to Stanford; the one expected to do great things with my fancy degrees. Except he'd been asking for several years now when I was going to get a job; when all the hard-earned money he'd put toward making me the first in my family to go to college (the scholarship, it turned out, didn't pay for housing or incidentals) was finally going to start paying off. It's the blue-collar parents' nightmare, I suppose, to work so hard to give their children opportunities, only to have their kids fall backward financially. My older brother, who'd become an electrician like our father and would someday take over the business, already had a house, a wife, and two kids.

"You'll read all about that, and all about him too," said Mrs. W—. She stopped outside a doorway. "Well, here we are."

The room we entered had once been a bedroom; there was still a daybed against one wall. A large wooden desk was set up by the window, which had a nice view of the back garden. There were four bookcases along the wall, opposite the daybed, but otherwise the room was quite bare. I wondered what had been here before, and if Mrs. W— had set it up as an office specifically for her project.

"My notebooks are in that bookcase," she said, pointing to a lower shelf of the bookcase closest to the desk. "Janet got through two of them, so you can start fresh with the third. You may use the computer—it is in the top drawer there. She left a folder, she said, with what she'd transcribed already. I don't know how those things work, but I trust that you do." She considered me again, and nodded. "Well, that will be all. You may begin."

"I may . . . what? I'm sorry, but . . . I have to go in a bit. I didn't realize I was starting today."

"Didn't Lourdes instruct you to be here at two o'clock?"

"Well, yes, ma'am." I couldn't believe I was calling this woman *ma'am*. "But I thought it was just to meet you."

"You could have done all of that and started your work too. You need to think ahead, young man."

I resisted the urge to defend myself. Who the hell did this woman think she was? And yet part of me felt properly chastised. She was right, I should have thought ahead. Again, I was too slow, too untuned to nuance to respond correctly to the situation at hand. And there was nowhere else I really needed to be.

Mrs. W— furrowed her brow. "Well, perhaps you can stay long enough to get a sense of the project. You can start looking through my journals—they can't leave the premises, of course. And you shouldn't have a problem reading them—my handwriting is impeccable—but if you have any questions, Lourdes can help. The terms of employment are the same for you as they were for Janet: ten hours a week, twenty-five dollars an hour, on days you arrange with Lourdes. She will pay you by check every two weeks. If anything changes in your schedule, we will need a week's notice. And I need you to sign the agreement."

"The agreement?"

"Yes, the confidentiality agreement. Any material information about my family you might find in the journals must remain private. Many people are curious about us, Mr. Nagano. And my enemies are always looking for information."

I couldn't imagine who her enemies might be, nor what they could possibly want to know. But scanning the one-page contract she put in front of me, I didn't see a problem with agreeing. I leaned over the desk and signed, then gave her back the document.

"Very good," she said. And then she was gone.

The sudden silence, after Mrs. W—'s stream of talk, was startling. For a moment I stood near the middle of the room, not moving. I felt strange, almost criminal, left alone in this house, in this room where her memories were housed. And now, looking around, I realized it wasn't as empty as I'd thought. There were several paintings on the walls, portraits of three blond people—two young men and a woman—in their late teens or early twenties. On another wall the three figures appeared again, this time in two group portraits. The paintings were oil, heavy, old-fashioned. Was this Mrs. W— in her youth? Were the two young men her brothers? If so, they all seemed flat and lifeless, and I wasn't sure if the effect was the result of an unskilled hand, or some essential dullness in the subjects themselves.

I pulled out the chair and sat down at the desk. When I took the laptop out of the drawer, I found a sticky note from Janet. *There's a folder on the desktop with the first two notebooks, saved as separate files. It totals about two hundred pages. Have fun!*

The bookcases were just to my left. They were empty except for an old printer wrapped in its cords and three stacks of Mrs. W—'s notebooks. Notebook, though, is a misleading term. These were books for writing, yes, but clearly handmade, with hardbound leather covers and heavy cream-colored paper, beautiful as objects in themselves. *Peabody & Dutton, 1922*, said the nameplate on the inside cover of one of them. *Stationers, Boston.* I wondered how much each of these books had cost, where they had originally come from, and how old they were. I was almost afraid that what I'd find inside would disturb their beauty.

There were two brown books on the right of one of the lower shelves, and I assumed these were the ones Janet had finished, but I had no way to know until I could check against the files on the laptop. It occurred to me that I should read through what Janet had already transcribed, but that would take time, and already it felt like I'd fallen behind. I needed to start from wherever Janet had left off. So I picked up the top notebook from the left-hand pile, laid it flat on the desk, and carefully opened the cover.

Inside was writing—printed writing, which was medium-sized and exact, blue ink from a fountain pen, as legible as Mrs. W— had promised. Her lines were perfectly straight even though the paper itself was not lined. There were also sketches, clippings, photographs pasted in—this was an album of her life. Flipping through, I saw pictures of an orange grove in what was now the San Fernando Valley, framed by the San Gabriel Mountains. There was a picture of the coastline of Malibu with just a few scattered shacks, not the glut of oversized modern houses there today. There was a photo of four young women at some kind of party; one of them looked vaguely like the girl in the oil painting. Each of the pictures had arrows pointing out certain features, with written explanations on the page. *One of Father's orange groves. The oranges were sour that year*, was one. *1952, before the riffraff took over Malibu*, said another.

I turned back to the front of the notebook, where the writing on the first page picked up in midscene. *Just like I told Clara, John was already there, making cow eyes at that hussy, Evie Johnson.* This was her account of a night at the Cocoanut Grove, where John—who had apparently broken off an engagement with Clara—was visibly courting the new *hussy*, and our heroine, young Marion, approached him on the dance floor and called him a horse's ass right in front of all their friends.

That this minor social escapade should be recorded in a journal seemed trivial to me, but as I went on, there was more of the same. For an hour I read accounts of other nights on the town—and once, of a wedding shower where Elizabeth Taylor had apparently had too much to drink. Mrs. W—'s accounts were documentary in tone, with little flashes of wit, but she seemed largely absent from them herself. What I mean is, she was in them, usually causing some sort of trouble, but the entries themselves were rather mundane.

At four o'clock, I closed the notebook and replaced it on the shelf. I shut down the laptop and pushed it to the back of the desk. This would be tedious work, but easy, and I was looking forward to the money. Silently I thanked Janet for hooking me up. Then I wandered out to the hallway and into one of the living rooms, calling out to Mrs. W—. She didn't appear, but another woman did. This woman was pretty, Latina, probably in her thirties, wearing a crisp black dress.

"Mrs. W— is taking her afternoon rest," said the woman. "Was everything all right? I'm Lourdes."

I wanted to ask her a thousand questions—how long had she been there? What was it like? Was she afraid to touch things, as I was? How did she keep from getting lost in the vast expanses of this house? But I held my tongue and said that I had everything I needed. In a friendly but no-nonsense way, Lourdes led me to the door. Then I stepped outside, and heard the door shut behind me. I was alone. I tried to reflect on what had happened in the last few hours, but it was all too much, too new. Instead, I just stood there for a minute. The entire city was laid out before me—Hollywood below, Downtown to the east, Santa Monica and Venice to the west, Palos Verdes and Catalina far off in the distance. The sun was gleaming off the ocean and the traffic was already clogging the freeways. But up here, Mrs. W— was above it all. I sighed, took one last look at the house, walked out to my car, and drove back down into the city.

CHAPTER TWO

That night I treated myself to dinner at my favorite Cuban restaurant—a big, noisy place on Venice Boulevard that served huge plates of pork, black beans, rice, and plantains. The food was cheap—ten dollars a plate—but I still wouldn't have sprung for it if I hadn't known a check was coming, and as it was I just drank water to save money. But I was feeling celebratory, the best I'd felt in weeks—not only at the prospect of making some money, but also because a door had opened to a new experience. Sitting there by myself, eating pork so tender and savory it almost brought tears to my eyes, hearing laughter and conversation all around me, I realized how narrow my life had become. For several years it had revolved around only two places—the apartment I shared with Chloe, and campus. But now that I was done with classes and didn't teach anymore, I had no reason to go to campus except the occasional torturous meeting with Professor Rose; and my place, without Chloe, was depressing and claustrophobic. I'd been treading water, trapped in a holding pattern. Days followed days that were so indistinguishable I lost track of what month it was.

Working on the dissertation more or less full-time had only made things worse. It wasn't just that I'd lost interest in my topic. I was starting to question the study of history itself. Mine was not the usual complaint of the underrepresented: that history is written by the victors, stories of everyday people are lost, etc. No, my problem was different. It was more that I didn't know where the past ended and the present began. I didn't know when something was *over* enough to isolate, capture, make statements about. If events of the 1800s affected the early twentieth century, and the results of that, in turn, led to changes fifty years down the road, then who's to say that it was ever really done? That we weren't, even today, simply playing out another chapter in a story that was nowhere near complete? And how could I, from some undefined middle part of the narrative, step back and make any kind of declaration? Especially when I didn't know how the events I was studying had any relevance to the present? History was taking shape all around us, in ways big and small, and it seemed fruitless, even arrogant, to try to capture it. It would be like pinning a butterfly into a specimen box while it was still alive and wriggling.

At least that's what I told myself. I could have been full of shit. It could have just been that I was looking for a reason not to do my work, and this line of thought sounded respectably existential. The truth was, I was going slowly nuts by myself in that apartment. And while the fact that I wasn't teaching did free up more time, that wasn't necessarily a good thing. Teaching had given me structure, something to get up and prepare for, and that had made me use my time carefully. But even more, it had given me a reason to interact with people. For all my tendencies toward solitude and self-pity, I loved to be in the classroom. I had the ability to entertain and amuse, as unasked for and inexplicable and unrelated to the rest of me as other people's talents for juggling or wiggling their ears. The intellectual exchange—but even more than that, the students' curiosity and hopefulness, their *energy*—had been stimulating and sweet and exciting enough to make me forget—at least for the hours I was there—about my own problems.

Now, I'd go two or three days at a time without leaving the apartment, living off cold pizza, not shaving, and only showering when it seemed indecent not to. Not that the world outside was so enticing. I lived in Jefferson Park, about two miles from campus, in a neighborhood of blue-collar workers, retirees, USC grad students, and a sprinkling of folks with no discernible profession. Our street was a mix of two- and four-unit apartments, a few Spanish-style homes, and lovingly maintained Craftsman houses. One end was anchored by a noisy twelve-unit building, the other by a moss-green, three-story Victorian beauty. There was no cohesion whatsoever—it was like the overflow buildings from more architecturally unified neighborhoods had been gathered and deposited here. The only common features were the burglar bars that covered every first-floor door and window, a nod to the area's enduring grittiness. The cars in the driveways were mostly worn sedans, with a couple of Beamers mixed in, and one classic, restored Chevy pickup. The yard of one house, occupied by a teenager taking care of his grandmother, was guarded by an old, tire-less Buick propped up on cinder blocks.

My building represented polyglot LA all by itself. The back unit was occupied by the owner, a black sixty-ish accountant, a widower. Above him was a quiet, middle-aged Mexican couple who always regarded me suspiciously. Directly below me was a white thirty-something USC law student and his Korean American wife; their seven-year-old daughter was the only child on our end of the block. Chloe and I were a mixture of mixes—me Japanese and Polish, her Japanese and black. And directly across from me was my old high school friend Kevin—the grandson of black sharecroppers from Arkansas who had made their way west—and his Dominican girlfriend Rosanna. Kevin, who worked as a paramedic with the Los Angeles Fire Department while he was studying to be a nurse, would try to get me to come over and watch the Lakers with him, but I usually begged off due to work. He was worried about my solitary, decrepit, woman-less state, but I insisted that I wanted to be left alone—and the truth was, his happy coupledom just rubbed salt in my hermitous wound.

Being alone, though, didn't mean I was productive. I avoided the pile of books on my desk as if they were a lover with whom I'd split but still shared an apartment. I might engage with them half-heartedly for an hour or two, but then I'd give up, choosing instead to thumb through a novel I lacked the attention span to read; or to watch the endless loud cycle of *SportsCenter*. I canceled my social media accounts when I caught myself checking on Chloe's pages, torturing myself with images of her looking happy at work, or with her friends, without me. I skipped meetings with my advisor and my dissertation support group. And I avoided seeing my family, even missing—it pains me to write this—my father's sixty-fifth birthday. There's not much I can say to account for my time between June of 2010 and January 2011. I watched more reality television than anyone should ever admit.

I drove back up to Mrs. W—'s house two days later. This time, I was greeted by Lourdes, who led me to the office and offered iced tea, which I declined, and said to call if I needed anything. She told me that Mrs. W— was out with her women's group and would probably not be back while I was there. She clarified that she, Lourdes, was Mrs. W—'s "personal assistant"—i.e., she took care of all her scheduling, shopping, and personal needs— and I was her "research assistant." There was also a housekeeper, the gardeners, two cooks, a chauffeur, and a butler. This seemed a bit much for one person.

"Mrs. W—, she's very attached to that book," Lourdes said, and it took me a moment to realize she meant the project I was working on. "She wants to make sure that things get remembered right. Especially about her father and grandfather."

"Well, why wouldn't they?"

Lourdes smiled indulgently. "People don't know much about the W— family. They've kept a low profile, and the things that have been said about them haven't always been true."

Something about the tone of her voice made me wonder what those people had said. It also made me wonder how long she'd worked for the W—s. Had she known Mrs. W— for much of her life? I wasn't sure it was acceptable to ask.

I settled down in the office, fired up the laptop, and opened the notebook I'd looked at two days before. It didn't take long to get through what I'd already read,

about the party at the Cocoanut Grove. This was followed by accounts of other parties, and of a hunting trip
to Jackson Hole. There, Mrs. W— went for a horseback
ride with the son of one of her father's friends, whose
name I'd also recognized from buildings in town. *Lars
S— just would not stay away from me with his hairy hands and
putrid breath*, she'd written. *I should have shot him in the woods
and called it a hunting accident.*

I'd been working steadily for two and a half hours—
I'd typed twenty pages—when I felt a presence behind
me. Turning around, I saw Mrs. W— standing in the
doorway. I had no idea how long she had been there.
She was dressed in a honey-colored pantsuit, cut fash-
ionably at the neckline, with an orange scarf, small pearl
earrings, and a thin necklace to match. It was a simple
outfit, yet nothing like the suits that businesswomen
wore—more unique, most likely individually tailored,
clearly something not off any rack. "Interesting stories,
aren't they?" she asked, ignoring my surprise.

"Yes," I said. "I just read about your father's going on
the board of the County Art Museum and how one of his
business rivals tried to keep him off." Then I stopped,
suddenly afraid it might not have been proper to comment. But she didn't seem to mind.

"Yes, Travis Jones," she said. "That backstabbing
crook. He kept a whore in Tijuana—who would go to
Tijuana anyway, except to find a whore? He eventually
died of syphilis."

She asked how many pages I'd typed that day, and
when I told her, she seemed pleased. "You're fast," she
said approvingly. Then: "I'm tired from talking to old
windbags. Come to the garden and have some iced tea."

I left my things and followed her to an outside seating area paved with blue polished stones and surrounded by a river rock wall. In the center was an iron and glass table and a matching set of chairs; around the edges, flower beds with flowers in spectacular bloom. The lawn extended out in every direction, lush grass not native to the chaparral hills. From the patio you could see the entire city—Downtown in the distance, the San Gabriel Mountains rising behind, the vast spread of Los Angeles in every direction. You could sit here and watch the sun rise over the mountains in the morning and see it set over the ocean at night. It was like the homestead of a conquering ruler—which, I supposed, is exactly what the W—s were.

We sat at the table and I kept rearranging myself, unsure of whether to sit up straight or lean back, cross my legs or keep both feet on the ground. Outside, I was reminded of the sheer scale of Mrs. W—'s home—from our spot, I couldn't see either end of it. Another young woman, whom Mrs. W— addressed as Maria, came out with a silver platter holding a pitcher and tall glasses. She set the glasses in front of us and poured the iced tea, being careful not to look us in the face. Mrs. W— smiled and thanked her. Now she sat drinking, back still straight, looking very much in her element. She'd put on a shawl that looked more fashionable than warm; I myself felt a bit of a chill. The moment before she slipped on her dark glasses, I caught a glimpse of her eyes, which were the blue of the ocean, the blue of the earth from space.

"Those women," she started midsentence, and I didn't know at first whom she was speaking of, "they sit around all day talking about parties and clothes, or where their families will summer this year. No interest in the larger world, in politics, in art. No wonder all their husbands have mistresses."

I lifted my glass with a shaky hand, praying I wouldn't spill it, and took a sip. It was like no iced tea I'd ever tasted. As if the herbs had been plucked straight from some heavenly garden and transported directly to my glass. "The women's group?" I ventured.

"Yes. We meet monthly to talk about raising funds for the children's hospital. When the group started fifty years ago, it had the very best girls in the city." And she named several names I recognized: governors' wives, names from department stores and international corporations, even one president's wife. "But now all of that's changed, and the younger girls just aren't the same caliber."

I didn't know what to say to this, and instead looked down at the Lhasa apsos, who'd shuffled over to a nearby patch of grass and were now rolling on their backs, wriggling and grunting with joy.

"They're ridiculous, aren't they?" Mrs. W— said. "I've always thought they looked like Winston Churchill."

"They're pretty funny," I offered.

"This is the third Pinot. The first two were eaten by coyotes. One they carried off right in front of me. A big coyote came and plucked him like a dandelion."

"That's terrible!" I said. "How'd it get in here?"

"They're crafty. Even six-foot-high fences can't keep them out. Now I resort to a rifle."

"You shoot them?"

"I told you already. I'm a very good shot."

We were silent for a moment, and I turned to take this all in—the land, the view, the coyote-bait dogs, the image of Mrs. W— with a gun. In an outer circle of the yard, I could see two of the llamas; at night they were brought into an outbuilding, and now I knew why. I picked up my drink again. The glass had left a ring of water on the cut-stone coaster, and I brushed it off hurriedly, and then didn't know what to do with my wet hand. Surreptitiously I wiped it on my pants. Now Mrs. W— looked at me and asked, "And what about you? What are you studying?"

Haltingly, I tried to describe my research, my classes, the subjects I'd taught.

"Have you enjoyed USC?" she asked.

I paused. Had I enjoyed it? I didn't really know. "Yes, I've had some very good professors," I said.

"Good. Every now and again we have to go through that place and clean out all the Commies."

I thought she was kidding. "Excuse me?"

"Those left-wingers that rule the universities now. But *you*," she said, tipping her glass at me, "you seem very sensible."

I wasn't sure whether to be flattered or insulted to be distinguished from the left-wing Commies.

"Those academics wouldn't recognize history if it bit them in the ass," she continued. "History doesn't happen in books. It happens *out here*." She tapped the table with her bony finger. "It bends to the will of important people."

She pulled a handkerchief from her pocket—it was embroidered with MW—and delicately patted her lips. I noticed her hands then—thin and graceful, no age spots or beauty marks, and while I did see a few delicate lines, they had the effect of making the skin look more lovely, the way that tiny cracks in porcelain can make one aware of the delicacy of the clay.

"My journals tell more of the history of Los Angeles than all those boring scholarly books put together," she said. "My grandfather Langley *made* this city. And yet so few people are even aware of it." Then: "You were talking about the County Art Museum. Well. This Sunday, the new north wing is being dedicated. Waverly Stone, that insufferable fool, donated her family's sculpture collection, but the building itself was funded by a fifty-million-dollar anonymous gift."

I didn't know what to say. What does one say about fifty million dollars? I could barely scrounge up fifty.

"You should come with me," Mrs. W— said. "It will help you understand the world you're reading about."

I sat up straight. "Mrs. W—, I've got things to do—my dissertation, and . . ." I stopped. What did I have to do, really? And besides, I was curious. Mrs. W— must have known this, because she said, "Come here at five o'clock. My driver will take us." Looking me up and down with an expression of distaste, she added, "We shall have to arrange to get you better clothes."

The next day, I found myself at a men's store on Robertson Boulevard, being tended to by Rafael, a tall, refined shadow of a man with sleek brown hair.

At first, Mrs. W— had planned to send me to Rodeo Drive, but after conferring with two of whom she called the "younger girls" in their forties about where they shopped for their husbands, she decided I needed clothing more appropriate for my age. She had waved off all protests by explaining again that this was related to my work. "It's no different than a job that requires a uniform," she said. "And the employer provides the uniform."

And so I turned myself over to Rafael, and watched in bewilderment as he brought over jackets, shirts, pants made with material I'd never heard of, things so soft and fine and pleasing to touch I was afraid to put them on. I owned a couple of jackets and a pair of decent trousers, but they seemed like ratty gym clothes compared to this finery. Rafael's ability to choose clothes that might suit me was utterly mysterious, like someone who could walk through a forest and see signs of animal life that were invisible to the untrained eye.

"Such a good-looking man," he said, not trying to butter me up, or to flirt, for that matter, but in a slightly chastising tone that suggested I wasn't doing very well with what I had. "You don't think very much, do you? About your clothes."

I had to admit I didn't, but when I tried on the outfits he brought in—nervous at first about tearing or soiling them—I was amazed at the transformation. The clothes that had appeared so untouchable on their hangers now seemed like they'd been made just for me. Looking in the mirror, I saw someone well-dressed and confident, a man of a certain standing. I didn't recognize who I was looking at.

At Mrs. W—'s instruction, we settled on two outfits— a dark-gray pinstripe suit with a white silk shirt and lavender tie, and tan trousers and a navy-blue jacket with a light-blue tie. Italian leather shoes to match each outfit, as well as pocket squares and two new leather belts.

I made a show of trying to pay for at least part of the purchase, which embarrassed us both. There was no way I could have afforded even a single shoe. With the accessories, the total bill was equal to about six months' rent.

Rafael slipped the clothes into a garment bag; then he handed me another bag that held the shoes and the belts. "Take care of these," he said, as if I couldn't be trusted with them. I muttered thanks and escaped to my car.

On Sunday afternoon, I drove up to Mrs. W—'s house, wearing the gray pinstripe suit. I felt self-conscious from the moment I stepped out my front door—first because of my neighbor, Mrs. Hernandez, who stared at me in shock, the water from her garden hose spilling onto her shoes; then because my beat-up Honda seemed inadequate for the occasion. Suddenly I understood why people cared about cars—they were the ultimate accessory, the first impression you created. An ugly car could nullify whatever was inside, like precious jewels encased in a layer of mud.

But luckily I wasn't going to the museum in my car. I was going to Mrs. W—'s. When I drove up, the Bentley was parked out front, and a driver in suit and cap was polishing the headlights. Mrs. W— came to the doorway, looked me up and down, and made a sound of general approval. "Rafael did very well," she said, after she'd made me turn a full circle. "I will have to send him a tip."

She herself looked marvelous in an elegant silver-green pantsuit and silver flats. She carried a small purse and shawl, and when I got a bit closer, I saw the subtle makeup, the perfectly styled hair. I also saw that she was holding a cane. It had a small round mirror attached to the bottom, and when she saw me notice this, she lifted the cane and shook the end of it. "For looking up women's dresses," she said. "You can always tell how classy someone is by the cut of her underwear."

When I helped her down the stairs, her grip on my arm was surprisingly firm. The driver opened the door and helped her in, and then I got in the other side. Other than a few times taking a cab, I'd never been in a car with a driver. I didn't know what to say, or where to hold my hands. But Mrs. W— and the driver, a fifty-ish black man named Dalton, talked a blue streak about, of all things, baseball. Mrs. W— was a very knowledgeable fan, with an attachment to the Dodgers. As much as she hated Rupert Murdoch—"a crook and a blowhard," she called him—she also said that the ownership of the Mc-Courts was proving to be a failure, because they'd structured the purchase of the team with so much debt. He would lose the team soon, she predicted. "If you can't buy something outright, you can't afford it at all," she said.

"Mrs. W—," said Dalton, chuckling, "the price was four hundred million dollars. Not too many people can afford four hundred million dollars."

"That's right!" she said. "And those who aren't rich have no business pretending that they are."

"Do you ever go to games?" I asked. I couldn't imagine her eating a Dodger dog and drinking a beer.

"Certainly not!" she replied. "I wouldn't subject myself to all of those loud, unruly people. They sweat. They fight. Really, the team should post immigration officers at the entrance gates and intercept all the illegals!"

I turned to the window to cover my surprise, but Dalton just chuckled. "Now, now, Mrs. W—. No need to be like that. They pay for their tickets like everyone else."

"Not their ticket into America," she said.

I wanted to say something, to counter, but I didn't have the easy rapport with her that Dalton did, so I sat in shameful silence. I wondered if Mrs. W— spoke this way in front of Lourdes and Maria. But I didn't have much time to think about it because we'd arrived at the museum, where Dalton pulled up in front, jumped out, and opened the door. He helped Mrs. W— out and I scrambled after her; when she gathered herself, she hooked her hand around my elbow. She lifted her head to the curious people, the cameras and lights, as if toward a warming sun.

What can I say about that night at the museum, the first of many events I attended with Mrs. W—? It was both daunting and thrilling, all the more surreal because it happened in a place I knew. I'd been to the museum before, to see major exhibits when they came through town, usually at the prodding of Chloe, who was always dragging me to cultural events I wouldn't have attended on my own. Yet I had never seen the museum like this, shut off from the public, reserved for a private party. And the other guests were not your typical weekend museum-goers dressed in sweaters and jeans and casual skirts. The people that night were in attire that I had never seen before, except in movies—the women in gorgeous cocktail dresses, the men in fine suits, and so many fancy necklaces and bracelets and earrings and watches that all the jewelry stores in Beverly Hills might have been raided for the occasion. Everyone looked somehow not just dressed up but untouched, like models of humans that seemed real but weren't quite; these were beings who never exerted themselves, never sweated, never dug in their gardens, never sullied themselves with laundry. Almost all of them had drinks in their hands—champagne or wine or cocktails—and they stood around small, raised tables with plates of hors d'oeuvres, served by young men and women in black suits and white shirts weaving through the crowd with their trays. Other than myself and a few of the servers, everyone in attendance was white. I followed Mrs. W—, who was stopped every few steps by someone who proclaimed how happy they were to see her—although many more saw her and looked away, in avoidance or what seemed like fear. Eventually we made our way up the concourse and into the courtyard of a new steel-and-glass building. There, maybe twenty human-size stone sculptures stood like sentinels in front of the windows. These, I was made to understand, were the donated sculptures, the occasion for that night's event. They were lovely, but my eyes were drawn past them to the building, which was lit from within, the three-story glass windows inviting one to enter.

Mrs. W—'s appearance stirred the crowd—people turned, cameras flashed, the clamor of voices dipped, then rose again. Through it all, Mrs. W— smiled grandly, and even though she was not particularly tall, her presence dominated the space. Two middle-aged couples appeared out of nowhere, blocking our way. They greeted Mrs. W— with an effusiveness that she did not return.

"Richard, dear," she said, when they turned their curious eyes to me, "this is Mr. and Mrs. Steve Birkhall, and Mr. and Mrs. John Grant. This is Richard Nagano. He's a graduate student finishing up his PhD in history at the university."

"A graduate student!" said one of the wives. They all seemed to know what Mrs. W— meant by *the university*. "I thought you were an actor!"

I blushed.

"Yes," Mrs. W— said, rescuing me. "Well, as we always knew, youth and beauty are wasted on the young." Then into my ear, a whisper that was loud enough for others to hear: "John Grant's business partner went to jail on an insider-trading scandal. If you ask me, Grant's as guilty as he was."

At that moment, someone from the museum pulled her over to an actual red carpet on the side of the courtyard with a large white backdrop that bore the museum's name and logo, as well as the names of two of the largest banks in town. Mrs. W— posed with one person, then another, including a couple of people who looked vaguely familiar, like actors in a well-received series on cable that hadn't been renewed for a second season. And while the other person in the shot always smiled at the camera, Mrs. W— looked into the lens with a sardonic expression, lips barely upturned, indulging the photographer and all the people who might view the photographs but not deigning to enjoy the attention.

I wandered over to the food tables, which were overflowing, lavish, laden with platters that held wheels of baked brie, slices of salmon, dollar-coin-sized white bowls of caviar. One skill I'd developed as a graduate student was a nose for free food, and this spread was the most extravagant I'd ever seen. There were plates of various meats sliced paper-thin, and skewers of delicate-looking vegetables and meat. There were mini-quiches, and bits of beef wrapped in arugula and bacon; and tiny bowls of lobster bisque. There were white popsicle sticks with round bits of cake on the end of them, frosted, and small glasses of colorful viscous fluid that the stand-up label identified as *fruit shots*. All of this was framed by a village of gingerbread houses, so large they could have been homes for the Lhasa apsos. They were decorated with colored frosting in curlicues around the windows and doors, disks of candy lining the roofs, waves of green frosting denoting shrubbery around the bottoms. Beside the tables on either side, two giant ice sculptures, which—when I looked more closely—were replicas of pieces in the sculpture collection. I stood in front of the table feeling slightly overwhelmed, not sure whether I should touch anything.

"It's a bit much, isn't it?" a voice said from near my left shoulder.

I turned to face a woman of about my age. She was standing so close I couldn't really see her. I fought the urge to pull away—her face was inches from my own—and answered, "Well, no one should go hungry."

"Except they will. Have you noticed? None of the women are eating."

I turned and scanned the long table, and it was true:

the only people hovering over the food trays were men. I looked out at the crowd and watched the waiters and waitresses with their platters of passed hors d'oeuvres; they seemed not to have many takers.

"Maybe they're waiting for dinner."

The woman laughed, throwing her head back a little, exposing her long, fine neck. This gave me a chance to move back just a little. "We could only hope," she said. "There's always so much waste at these things, it's shameful. I've tried to get the committee to donate the leftover food, but they won't do it. The caterer doesn't want to be associated with giving handouts."

"The committee?"

"The events committee. The brilliant minds who put this together."

With the bit of space between us, I was able to look at her now. She was nearly my height—5'10"—but a good three inches of that was heels. She wore a sleeveless, champagne-colored dress that would have hugged her nicely, except there wasn't much figure to hug. For all her talk of women not eating, it didn't look like she ate much herself. There was some kind of brown pattern sewn into her dress, and her shoes and purse matched it perfectly. The whole getup was expensive and classy; I didn't know that women of my general age group could dress like this. Her face was made up impeccably, but not overdone; she'd worked hard to make herself look natural. She had fine patrician features, smooth planes of cheek and an aquiline nose, a forehead that was entirely free of wrinkles. Her blond hair had been swept back from her face and gathered by some device I couldn't see. She wore dark, almost blood-colored lipstick on lips surprisingly full for such a wisp of a woman. Her look was completed with a string of pearls and hard, bright earrings. Everything about her made me want to keep looking. And yet I couldn't really say if she was pretty.

"I'm Fiona Morgan," she said, holding out her hand, but with her elbow still bent at her side. The hand was long and bony and her skin was silk-soft, but her grip surprisingly strong. Her posture was perfect. It made me want to stand up straighter myself.

"I'm Rick—Richard—Nagano," I said.

"It's a pleasure to meet you, Richard. It's nice to see some new blood at these things. I can't tell you how tired I am of seeing all the same faces. That man over there—" she pointed at someone, but I couldn't tell which of several blue-suited men she was referring to, "that's Paul Wilkensen. I've seen him at three events just this week alone." She leaned in. "That's wife number three, and number two is also here, with his former business partner."

A waiter appeared behind us with a big platter of meat; he somehow held it aloft while lifting the old one, which was only half-empty, and then placed the new one down.

"You must go to a lot of events," I said. I was noticing the curve of her cheekbone, the line of her elegant jaw.

She sighed. "Yes, well, my family's been involved with just about every major institution in town. The museum, Los Angeles Music Center, USC, the Huntington, blah blah blah. It's funny. I don't even *like* art. Or museums, anyway. They seem so oddly stilted." She was quiet for a moment, and when she tucked a strand of hair back behind her ear, I saw the huge diamond ring she wore and the platinum-and-diamond wedding band. Then she turned back to me, head tilted, chin jutting, looking at me cockeyed. "But that's all boring. What about you? What are you doing here tonight?"

"I came as a guest of Mrs. W—'s," I said. I wasn't sure how much to reveal.

"Marion, of course! So you're her latest walker."

"Walker?"

"Escort. Platonic escort. For ladies who need a date. Most of the older widowed ladies have gentlemen walkers their own age. But Marion likes to bring young men—usually ones she knows through her art and fashion worlds, fabulous gay boys who properly worship her. You don't strike me as that type."

"None of the above."

"Well, lucky for us," Fiona said. She gave me a bright, exaggerated smile. Was she flirting? Being sarcastic? The norms here were so different that I couldn't tell.

"I'm actually doing some work for her. Research, you could say."

"Really. Are you involved with a think tank or a policy institute?"

"No, I'm a graduate student."

"A graduate student," she repeated. And now she gave me a look I couldn't quite decipher. "You seem so put-together for a student. What's your field?"

"Twentieth-century California history," I said. I didn't tell her that I looked so *put-together* because of Mrs. W—. "I'm ABD. No classes anymore, or teaching either. I'm just trying to finish my dissertation."

"And what's your topic?"

"Oh," I said, feeling self-conscious, "it's a bit obscure. You wouldn't find it interesting."

"Yes, I would!" Fiona exclaimed, with such enthusiasm that a man looked over from in front of the salmon plate, spatula of fish in his hand. "I'm a bit of a history nerd myself. Try me."

"Well, okay," I began, feeling the dread I always did when I had to talk about my work with a stranger. "I'm writing about Japanese prefectural associations called *kenjinkai* and their role in the early Japanese American community here in LA. People would come to the States and feel isolated, and then form these groups with other people from their home prefectures in Japan. Prefectures are kind of like states in America."

"Are you half Japanese?" Fiona asked.

"Yes."

"I thought so! That particular mix always seems to turn out well."

I blushed and stammered a thank you, which made her grin. "I'm writing specifically about the revolving credit mechanism that some of them established. Because banks wouldn't let Japanese immigrants open accounts, these guys would pool their money and advance capital for business and personal needs." I didn't mention that this was how my grandfather got his start.

"That's fascinating," Fiona said. "Really, what an interesting subject."

"Well, not really, but thank you." I felt a bit exposed, though also, in truth, more than a little flattered by her interest.

"But how did you connect with Mrs. W—?"

"I was recommended by the person who was working for her before. And I needed the job." I felt embarrassed to admit my financial straits in these opulent surroundings. But if Fiona registered the huge gulf between this setting and my reality, she didn't show it.

"You work out of her house in Bel Air?"

"Yes, three days a week. I've only just gotten started."

"She's quite a character, isn't she? I've always appreciated her lack of bullshit. It's such a rare quality in my circle."

I didn't know what to say now, so I turned toward the crowd, which was milling about the courtyard, some people looking at the statues, others standing around holding cocktails and admiring the new wing and its lit-glass entrance.

"Funny that Marion should come to *this*, though" Fiona said. "She despises Waverly Stone."

"Who?"

"The woman who donated the sculptures."

"Why?"

She shrugged. "Who knows? It goes way back; I think their fathers hated each other. Probably their grandfathers too—they battled over oil and land a hundred years ago. There's only so much room for the truly important in LA. It's really more like a small town in that way, with so few established families." She paused. "Not that there's anything to like about Waverly Stone."

"Mrs. W— mentioned something about a new wing being dedicated too."

"That's right. The modern art wing. No one knows who the donor is. That's probably why Marion came tonight—to see Waverly Stone get upstaged."

"Are you keeping some hungry young artist from his

dinner?" someone asked in a booming voice. We both turned to face a tall, blond, broad-shouldered man with a thin, drawn-in woman at his side.

"I'm doing nothing of the sort," Fiona said, smiling. "We're talking about history. And art."

"Bryson Rutherford," said the man, thrusting his hand toward me. I took it, and felt the bones in my own hand crush together. "This is my wife Michelle."

"Hello. Richard Nagano," I said, shaking the wife's much gentler hand. I wasn't sure of the proper way to greet these people, and watched with interest as Fiona and Bryson kissed each other cursorily on the cheek, and then as the women touched cheeks and fussed over each other's dresses and hair, like two bright butterflies fluttering together in some strange elaborate dance.

Rutherford looked me up and down, and it was not a friendly assessment. His skin was blotched red with anger or alcohol; his lips were set in a slight grimace; his small eyes had a coldness that his fine blue suit and gold cuff links could not disguise. "So you are an artist, aren't you?" he said. "You look like that type."

I wasn't sure what he meant by this, but it didn't improve my stock in his eyes when I responded, "No, I'm a graduate student."

"A graduate student!" he snorted. "Graduate school is a holding tank for people who can't make it in the real world. Except for business school and law school, of course."

"Bryson, don't be such an ass," Fiona said. "Rick's working on really interesting things. It's been fun to talk to someone who actually has a brain instead of having the same old conversations with *these* people."

Rutherford narrowed his eyes and glared at her. I remembered the time that Chloe had taken one look at a sportscaster when we were watching a ball game and said, *That is a man who beats women.* She'd been right—he was arrested a few months later for domestic battery. This guy had the same air of incipient violence, the same tension behind the veneer. Beside him, his wife seemed to shrink further. I was scared for Fiona but she just grinned up at him, charming, and his shoulders lowered an inch.

"Very funny, Fiona. You always did have quite a sense of humor."

Just then, Mrs. W— turned from the group she'd been standing with. I saw her looking for me, saw her eyes settle on my face. She gestured for me to come over, and I did, Fiona a step behind.

"I thought I'd lost you, young man," she said pleasantly. Then, in a different tone, "Hello, Fiona."

"Hello, Marion," Fiona replied, bowing a bit; her cocksureness and defiance of just a moment before was gone; there was a hesitance I couldn't decipher. But then again, Mrs. W— seemed to inspire that in people. "You look lovely this evening."

"As do you," said Mrs. W—. "The color suits you. Is your husband with you this evening?"

"No, he's working," said Fiona. "They're trying to close a new deal. You know Aaron. I can't tear him away from his job."

"He's done very well for himself," Mrs. W— remarked. "And so have you."

"Yes, indeed," said Fiona. She blushed.

"Well, Richard and I are going to move along. Please give my regards to your mother."

"I will," said Fiona. And then, waving to me, she disappeared back into the crowd.

The ceremony was dull and went on for too long; three stuffy-looking men in dark suits made speeches, followed by a woman in a remarkable blue hat, a wide, veil-trimmed creation that might have been worn by a film diva in the 1930s. She appeared to have something to do with the committee that Fiona had mentioned, and it was she who presented the award of thanks, a miniature of one of the sculptures, to Waverly Stone, who looked—just as Fiona had advertised—highly unpleasant. She was underdressed for the occasion, wearing slacks and a flowing brown top of the type favored by women who are a bit too heavy, which she was. Yet it was her face that was truly unattractive, not because anything was wrong with the features especially, but because the expression—despite her fleshy cheeks— was somehow pinched, her lips curled slightly, as if she smelled something bad. This impression of distaste was magnified by the way that she stood—her head drawn back and in defensively, looking out with suspicion. She accepted her acknowledgment without a smile, and did not make eye contact with the presenter, or anyone in the crowd for that matter, and when someone tried to bring her to the microphone, she said, "No, absolutely not. I *told* you I wasn't speaking!" loud enough for her protest to be picked up by the mic.

"That Waverly Stone," said Mrs. W— beside me, rather loudly. "Well, no one ever accused her of being classy."

Then the same fancy-hat lady came back to the mic and talked about the new wing, the architecture, the anonymous donor, and as she spoke the lights of the courtyard went out, leaving only the new building and its grand three-story lobby in lights, like a beacon in the darkness; like a brilliant new planet. The effect was dramatic, and there were gasps.

". . . and the fact that this was made possible by the generosity of an *individual*," the lady said, "someone who is driven not by a need for recognition, but by a love of art, and a commitment to social institutions in Los Angeles, well, that is truly remarkable. We cannot know who this donor is, or if he or she is even with us tonight. But whoever it is, please know that the museum, our patrons and members, and indeed the entire city, are forever in your debt."

It was a bit over the top, and I could see why Waverly Stone might be annoyed. Who wouldn't be if they donated something worth untold millions only to be upstaged by some invisible rival? These games were beyond my ability to understand—competitions of an entirely different world.

Mrs. W— was nodding through all of this; she seemed pleased by the proceedings. Though when the ceremony was over and people were invited to tour the new building, she declined.

"I've seen what I came to see," she said. "I can tour the building later, when all these damned people are gone."

On the ride back to Bel Air, Mrs. W— was quiet at first. She gazed out the window, serene. I didn't know what to say and so chose to say nothing, until she turned and asked, "What did you think?"

"Of the event? It was nice," I said stupidly. "The sculptures were impressive, and the new building was beautiful." I wondered if I'd said the wrong thing by complimenting the sculptures, but she didn't seem to care.

"When they turned the lights out and all you could see was the new building, that was lovely, don't you agree?"

"I do." Then, because I wanted to know, because I couldn't help myself: "Who is that young woman I was talking with? Fiona Morgan?"

"Fiona," Mrs. W— repeated, still looking out the window. "I've known her all her life. Her last name is really Harrington. Morgan's her married name. She married a highly successful commercial real estate developer who's responsible for many of the new buildings in town. I don't think they see each other much. He's always working, and she flits about to lunches and events. She has a child, a nervous young thing. I'm not sure she sees him much, either."

"She mentioned that her family has something to do with the museum?"

"Indeed. Her mother's a board member, and served as president for a while. Fiona comes from very good stock, you know. The Harringtons are amongst the oldest families in the city. They owned the company that supplied steel to build tracks for the railroads, and they used to own much of Pasadena. Her grandfather was one of President Reagan's closest friends."

"Really."

"Yes, they've always been very involved in politics and the arts. Fiona herself was a talented dancer, but she gave that up to go into investment banking. She simply wasn't cut out for finance, though. For the last several years she's been tending to family concerns."

I sensed that by *family concerns* she didn't mean her husband and home life. "She seems to share your opinion of Waverly Stone," I said.

"She's a sensible girl. Always has been—there was a time . . ." She trailed off for a moment. "There was a time when I would see her quite often."

I was filing all this information away, trying to make sense of it. "It was nice to talk with her. I think she enjoyed the speculation around the anonymous donor."

"I enjoyed it too."

"Do you have any guess as to who it was?"

"I don't *have* to guess. I know." She turned from the window to face me; the passing streetlights illuminated her eyes. "It was me."

"It was—*what?*" I almost fell forward out of the bench seat and onto the floor of the car. "*You* gave that money?"

"Why, yes. Several years ago. No one there has any idea. They all think I'm a stingy old bitch."

I let this news sink in. Of course she had given it. That was the reason she'd wanted to attend. "But . . . why would you do that? Why wouldn't you want people to know?"

"I have no use for all this fuss," she said. "People groveling and then wanting more. It's better they think that you won't give them anything." She paused. "Plus it was a hoot to see Waverly so tortured, don't you think? She was beside herself, and didn't know who to be mad at. Ha ha ha ha ha!"

There was genuine pleasure on her face; I wasn't sure

whether to admire her act or to find it slightly mad. Now I turned and looked out the window myself, watched the lights on Wilshire, then on Sunset, as we headed back west. We wound up through the dark streets of Bel Air and back to the house; there Dalton helped Mrs. W— out of the car and we both walked her to the door.

"Good night, gentlemen," she said just before she disappeared. Then the door closed in our faces and she was gone.

CHAPTER THREE

The next morning I drove to campus to meet with my advisor, Professor Victoria Rose. I was feeling a bit groggy. I hadn't slept well; all night my mind was buzzing with images from the night before. I'd been tempted to postpone the meeting again, but knew it wouldn't be smart. We'd already tried to reschedule a couple of times after I'd canceled for my first day at Mrs. W—'s, and I hadn't tried very hard to find a new date. But she'd pressed it—it had been more than three months by this point; we hadn't met since mid-October—and I knew that when we did talk, the conversation wouldn't be easy. In an effort to account for the months I'd been out of touch, I'd spewed out twenty pages which I'd sent ahead of time, but they were sloppy, not deeply reasoned out, the research jammed in sideways. I knew Professor Rose would not be pleased; I entered her dark, cavernous office and sat in the heavy hard-backed chair—known to students as the Throne of Pain—as if offering myself up for punishment.

The room felt like an intimidation chamber. The floor-to-ceiling built-in bookshelves were stuffed with perfectly arranged books, and there were sliding wooden ladders on both sides. The massive wooden desk, with its thick claw feet and intricately carved edges, looked like it had been commandeered from some castle. The

Throne of Pain itself had been preserved, students whispered, from the home of the first governor of California after statehood. On the two walls without bookcases, there were framed posters of various academic conferences that listed Professor Rose as a keynote speaker, and not a few photos of Professor Rose herself—with past mayors of both political parties, receiving awards; with three different governors and a senator. Everything here seemed designed to emphasize both her prominence and your own insignificance.

I watched Professor Rose furrow her brow as she looked at my pages and wondered how bad it would be. She was better dressed than most professors; in her silk blouse, gray blazer, and bright but tasteful accessories, she looked like she'd just stepped off the set of a morning cable show, which in fact, that day, she had. Her rectangular-framed glasses slid down her nose a fashionable inch; a few loose strands of her auburn hair, which was tied into a ponytail, fell onto her cheeks, where they tangled with the pen she was forever trying not to chew. The tip of it would hover at her lips, and then—maybe when she came across some particularly offensive line—she'd lose the battle and bite down on the end of it, hard.

"This connection, between the rise of German nationalism and the racial covenants in the US? I'm not sure I buy it. The covenants did come into existence after World War I, but I don't know that they had any relation to what was happening in Europe. What are you basing this on?"

I looked at her, trying to keep a straight face, feeling the hard wood on my ass. The truth was, I had based it on nothing. I'd just written it because it sounded like a plausible theory. "The Ottenheim papers," I struggled. "They suggest that such covenants were being formalized in Germany, and it's possible that German immigrants brought the idea to Los Angeles."

She tilted her head just slightly, looking at me down her nose, as if wondering if I was trying to pull one over on her or if I really was that stupid. "Rick," she said, "I *know* the Ottenheim papers. I don't know how you'd draw that conclusion." She sighed, bit her pen again, and then set it down on her desk rather hard. "Is this all you've produced since the last time we met?"

A chill formed inside me, an ice cube melting at the bottom of my gut. "Well, Professor Rose, I've been toying with a number of theories. I keep taking steps in one direction and then moving into another. I—"

"It worries me, Rick. Your initial idea and even the first couple of chapters of this project were original and strong. But it seems like you've just petered out."

"I . . ." I didn't know what to say. Through the window, I could hear students out on the quad, playing Frisbee and blasting music and just enjoying the kind of late-winter day—seventy degrees in early February—that made the rest of the country hate California.

"It's not uncommon for grad students to hit a bump when they're ABD. The loss of structure with the end of coursework, and even being freed from teaching, gives students more time than some of them can handle."

"It's been a bit of an adjustment, but I don't think it's that."

"I don't think so either, Rick, and that's why I'm

worried. You seem truly *stuck*—like you've lost interest in the project."

"Well, that's not it, exactly."

"And these things can take on their own momentum, you know. Like a death spiral. Once you get sucked downward, it's almost impossible to pull out. I've seen this happen with several of my most promising students."

The ice cube had grown into a full-fledged iceberg, and was now moving up through my gut and chest, chilling me and cutting up my organs.

"The other problem," Professor Rose went on, and now she put the pages down and tapped her fingers on the surface of the desk, "is your Blain fellowship. It's supposed to be for two years, and the second year is contingent upon your performance during the first. But based on your work thus far this academic year, I don't think I can recommend you for a renewal."

Now I sat up straight, alarmed. "Professor Rose, it's not as bad as all that. There's more I can show you—this isn't all that I've done. I've written quite a few more pages." Quickly I calculated how long it would take to draft another chapter. If I really motored, I could hustle something up in a week.

She shook her head and waved her hand as if batting away a fly. "If this is the best of what you've got, then I don't think additional pages will help."

Outside, a delighted shriek from a female student. There was a splashy thud, and then another, the sound of water balloons breaking. Now a male voice shouting, "I'll get you! I'm going to get you back!" And then more laughter, fading as the students moved farther down the quad. Inside me the iceberg was sinking now, and I felt my shoulders sag. What would I do if I lost my funding? Would I lose the stipend from the university too? How would I be able to finish my dissertation? How the hell would I support myself?

Professor Rose closed her eyes and sighed. She reached under her glasses to rub her eyes, and in the moment that her eyes were uncovered, I could see that she was tired. She wasn't trying to be a hard-ass. I'd just royally fucked up. Now she pulled a piece of paper out of another pile and wrote something on it. I tried to read it upside down without being obvious. Did it have to do with the fellowship?

"Rick, what have you been doing for the last few months? For this whole year, really?"

"I don't know, Professor Rose. There's been a lot going on."

"I'm sure there has, but we *all* have a lot going on. There's just no excuse for this lack of productivity. My assessment to the Blain Foundation is due in two weeks, and I'm sorry, but you've given me no reason to recommend a renewal."

Panic rose up within me now. "But Professor Rose—"

"I'm sorry, Rick. It's nothing personal. It's just that there are so many other students, *productive* students, who could really use this support."

"Can you give me those couple of weeks?" I asked frantically. "You said it was due in a couple of weeks."

She sighed again. "Yes, but as I just explained, if what you're doing is along the same lines as what I've just seen, it isn't going to make any difference."

Her pronouncement fell between us like a sandbag.

I lowered my eyes. Outside, I heard another burst of laughter on the other side of the quad, over closer to the science building. The W— science building. I raised my head.

"Actually, I'm working on something totally different." I hadn't known I would say this until it was out of my mouth.

Professor Rose looked at me with a weary expression. She had heard so many excuses. "What?" She sounded impatient. "What are you talking about?"

"Something new, *completely* new, and no one's ever done it." I leaned toward her now, grabbing onto a line of hope, pulling myself up, fist after fist. "A different angle on the history of early LA." I peered right into her skeptical eyes. "I recently got access to some very interesting papers. The private papers of Marion W—."

Professor Rose furrowed her brow again, with mild interest now. "Marion W— of the W— family?"

"Yes! You know, the W— wing at the Natural History Museum. The W— Science Hall right here at USC! She's the granddaughter of Langley W—. And she's an important figure in her own right too."

Professor Rose tilted her head and looked at me intently. I wasn't sure she'd ever really looked at me before. "And what are these . . . papers you've found?"

"Her private journals. From when she was a girl, all the way until the present day. She writes about her father and grandfather, and some of their business dealings. She writes about other important LA people too."

"And how did you happen to come across these journals?"

"I . . . know the family," I said, not sure of how much

to reveal. Janet would never have mentioned her job with Mrs. W— to her professors at USC, and with her focus on Renaissance France, she had no dealings with Professor Rose or any of the other Americanists. I saw no reason why I should disclose it, either.

"And they've granted you access to them?"

"Yes, I have full access, but they never leave her house. I mean, she isn't sharing them with anyone else."

Professor Rose leaned back in her chair. She took off her reading glasses and set them on the table; I saw in her hazel eyes the stirrings of excitement. "That *is* interesting," she said. "The W—s have not cooperated with any attempts to document their story. They won't talk to the media, and they've never authorized any biographies. There's very little in terms of primary source material. Everything about them in historical accounts of LA is taken from public record, a few interviews with people who knew them, and a lot of speculation. Even the buildings you mentioned were named decades ago, in Langley's time. Marion W— has been almost totally under the radar."

I nodded, and gulped; it occurred to me that Professor Rose knew much more about the W—s than I did. Of course she did; I should have anticipated that. She had the advantage of three decades of reading and writing about California. But I had Mrs. W—.

"Langley W—," Professor Rose mused, more to herself than to me, "was one of the biggest oil and land barons of the early twentieth century. He helped found some of the most exclusive neighborhoods in Los Angeles. He handpicked several mayors. His oil holdings extended from LA to Kern County to Riverside." She crossed her legs and swiveled a quarter-turn in her chair, brought her hand up to her chin and tapped it with one finger. She was looking past me now, over my shoulder, out the door, out at history.

"It's highly irregular, of course, for a student to change topics altogether at this juncture of his graduate career. But this is an extraordinary circumstance." Now she dropped her hand and brought her leg down and leaned over the desk. "If you could find something, if you reveal new information about the family and their early dealings in the city, now *that* would be historically significant. It could unlock new truths about the legacy of the W—s, about the origins of Los Angeles!"

I sat back just a little. "I'm not sure, Professor Rose. I'm not sure there will be anything in the papers I have that would refer to early LA. I mean, these are Mrs. W—'s papers. You're talking about her grandfather."

She waved me off. "I know, I know, but maybe there's *something*. And if Marion W— kept all her papers, maybe there are other papers. Maybe her grandfather kept records or letters. Maybe her father did too."

That was possible—but it didn't mean I'd ever have access to them, or that Mrs. W— would ever tell me about them. "Maybe. But right now I only have *her* papers."

I could see Professor Rose making an effort to contain herself. "Well, it's a place to start. And it sounds like much more than we've ever had access to before."

I noted the *we*—the entitlement of historians, the co-opting of a student's findings by the professor who oversees him, the assumption that private records are naturally the province of a waiting and interested public.

"Well, I can see," I said. "I can see if there's anything in her writings. And maybe that will lead to something else."

"Maybe it will. Maybe it will." Professor Rose was alert now; her straight posture, her eyes, even the tapping of her pen, all betrayed her excitement, that historian's bloodlust, like a hunting dog that's just picked up a juicy scent. It occurred to me that any new insights into the W—s might benefit her as well. She held a distinguished professorship, but maybe she longed to become a dean, and maybe her student's accomplishment could help.

"Listen," she said, leaning farther over the desk, "if you figure this out, if you find something about the early fortunes of the W— family, this goes beyond just a dissertation. This would be the most exciting new development in the history of Los Angeles that we've had for many years."

"So . . ." I started stupidly, "does that mean you might still be willing to recommend me for the fellowship?"

She looked at me, blinked quickly, then laughed. "The fellowship! Yes, of course, with this lead, if you can pull it off, I'd recommend you for a renewal of your fellowship. But this is much bigger, Rick. That's what I'm trying to tell you. This could be a *book*. And the ticket to a job. Hell, we might even hire you here at USC!"

My heart was pounding and my hands were sweating; I was feeling a bit of whiplash. I'd gone from losing my fellowship to practically being offered a job in the space of ten minutes. "Well, what do you want to see before you write the recommendation?" I asked.

"You've got two weeks," she said. "Bring me something. Bring me something interesting about the W—s. Just a piece of information that hasn't been out there before—an anecdote, a quote, a bit of history—and that'll be enough to give me the confidence that you'll produce something special over the next year."

I gulped and thought for the first time about what I had done. Instead of just typing up Mrs. W—'s journal, I'd be trying to convince her to let me write about her family. For a second I felt a wave of guilt for bringing the W—s up with Professor Rose. But then I thought of the alternative—losing my fellowship, losing everything. Living on Top Ramen and grocery-store bagels, and the shame of admitting failure to my family. Mrs. W— was my only way out.

And besides, maybe I didn't really need to go down this path. I could give Professor Rose an interesting tidbit or two right now, to prove that I had access to the papers. But then, I could just pretend to look into Mrs. W—'s family. Doing that would at least buy me another year of funding, and in that time I could get back to work on my *real* topic. I wouldn't really be violating a confidence, I told myself. I was just playing the card that I had.

Over the next few days, I found out everything I could about the W— family. I started on the Internet, where a search returned only about forty references to Mrs. W—'s grandfather, Langley, and fewer about Robert, her father. As Professor Rose had said, very little had been written about the family directly; most of what I found were references in the biographies of other men. I found these books deep in the archives of the USC library, as well as old, yellowed copies of the *Herald-Examiner* and the *Los Angeles Times*. From these various sources, I learned that the W—s were an old New Hampshire family— mostly farmers, including Langley's father, James, who'd hired himself out to work on other people's property and never owned land himself. Langley had come to California in 1898 to join a distant cousin who had a position on a ranch near Fresno. After two years of chasing ranch jobs up and down the state, he settled in Southern California, where he worked as an oil driller for a couple of established companies, and then managed to buy, in those early preboom days, a small plot of land in Los Angeles. That plot did produce some oil—but it was the duller, brown, unscenic land he purchased in Kern County that led to the explosion of Langley's wealth, for on that Central Valley land, 130 miles north of Los Angeles, a massive new oil field was discovered—oil to fuel the burgeoning industries of automobiles and trains; oil that helped spur the growth of Southern California and the western half of the United States. With investment capital from a pool of donors, Langley bought more oil- rich lands, invented and distributed a new kind of drill bit sharpener, purchased a stake in a company that built a pipeline to the ocean—and quickly became one of the richest men in the state. He bought property in what eventually became Beverly Hills, Santa Monica, Palos Verdes, and Newport, quintupling his investment when those areas were developed. At the age of thirty, he built a huge estate just off of Sunset Boulevard, in what were then the outskirts of the city.

He was also, at least according to these accounts, a decent man—he hired other young men who'd traveled out from his hometown, and was known, even after he'd grown unimaginably rich, to grab a shovel at a work site and join his men. He gave prodigious amounts of money to various causes, particularly orphans and veterans, and eventually became a board member and large donor of the university where I was now languishing. In the two pictures I found of him in the *Los Angeles Times*, he looked handsome and like a bit of a swashbuckler—hair surprisingly long, sweeping mustache, and a glint in his eye that suggested there was either a bottle of whiskey or a pretty and possibly unclad woman just outside the camera's range. He'd suffered from heart problems, though, and had finally succumbed to a heart attack at sixty-eight, as if so much life, lived so intensely, had overwhelmed his system.

His son Robert had been cut from a different cloth. The heir to a fortune he'd had no part in creating, he made savvy, self-serving decisions—subdividing and selling off parts of the family's coastal properties, and continuing the development of several of the family's Westside holdings. But he'd had a conflict with his father over the oil business—he'd wanted to take it public rather than keeping it in the family—and more personal differences too. Whereas Langley was big-spirited, down to earth, and gregarious, Robert was calculated and reserved. Langley took plenty of risks and failed as often as he succeeded, and the wealth that resulted from his better bets seemed like a bonus, not the point. But for Robert, the inheritor, preserving and expanding wealth was his life's occupation, and there was nothing fun or adventurous about it. Several articles— old, yellowing *Los Angeles Times* pieces I was thrilled to hold in my hands—described Robert as *merciless* or *a ruthless businessman, unconcerned with human consequence if a profit was at stake.* In his pictures—and there were more of them than there had been of his father—he was clean-cut and straight-backed, dark hair combed severely off his forehead. He was always posed formally, in a suit and tie, unsmiling. He looked, to tell the truth, like a stick in the mud.

And yet this was the man that Mrs. W— adored, and in whose eyes she'd been the proverbial apple. Their bond must have been even more intense because of the other thing I learned from my research—that Robert's other child, and only son, had died at eighteen.

This was news to me; Mrs. W— hadn't mentioned a sibling. But she'd had a brother, named Langley after his grandfather, three years older than her. Langley had died his freshman year at USC of unexplained causes, leaving fifteen-year-old Marion in effect an only child, living with her parents in their mansion in Bel Air. Her mother, Barbara, was the daughter of another oil family; other than two references to her charity work, there was nothing of her in the books or the papers. I wondered if the closeness with her father Mrs. W— spoke of was largely forged from this time. It occurred to me that I should read the first two hundred pages of Mrs. W—'s memoir, which must have included these sad events.

There was plenty of mention of Mrs. W— herself in public record, where she was identified as her father's only heir when he died, and some news stories connected her to the sale of her family's oil holdings, which had made her a billionaire. But most accounts of her were in the old society pages of the *Los Angeles Times*. The first reference was from 1952, when she was sixteen, announcing her debutante party. The girl in this picture stunningly resembled the woman I'd meet more than fifty years later. The face was a girl's face, fresh and more open—but the haughtiness was the same, as well as a quality in her expression, something sardonic and more than typically self-aware. This expression stayed consistent through her early twenties, as she was escorted to various social events by a succession of wealthy young men, some of whose family names I recognized, before marrying— in 1960—Baron J—, himself the heir of another of California's royal families, the son of an timber magnate, and also a decorated pilot in the Second World War. I recognized Baron's family name—it graced a number of buildings around town. There was a series of photographs of the J—s looking young, handsome, and untouchable, attending various functions. They had three children in eight years—two boys and a girl—and Baron was brought into the W— family business. All seemed to be going well until 1968, when Baron, who was sixteen years older than Mrs. W—, contracted a rare form of brain cancer and was dead within months. And there was Marion, a widow at thirty-two, with three small children to raise by herself.

There was little mention of Mrs. W— in the press for several years, except in the obituaries of her parents, who died just months apart, where she was listed as the sole surviving child. Then there was a rather salacious story from 2002 involving her youngest son, who'd been caught in some kind of after-hours club, much to the clucking of the *Times'* society editor, in the company of a disreputable woman. When Mrs. W— did appear again, she'd resumed using her family name, which caused a stir in itself, and the tone of the stories was different. They were mostly about her appearances at charity functions, or her fashion sense, or her growing collection of expensive modern art. There was an article about a commercial real estate development in Malibu in which she was a partner, and another about her family foundation. But anything remotely personal or revealing was wiped clean—an erasure or obfuscation that was aided by the demise of the society section.

Staring at my computer late at night, or sitting hunched over a desk at the library, I felt both full and unsatisfied, glad to be sorting through this trove of information, but unsure of what exactly it meant. As with all written history, what intrigued me the most was what was left out of the record. What had it been like for young Marion to grow up with such a humorless father? How had her brother died? Why did she never remarry? And why, after the one article about her youngest son's debacle, was there no mention of her children?

I wanted to talk to someone, but there was no one to approach: no scholar who had insight into the W—'s story, no journalist who'd written an account. Of course, the one person I could have asked was Janet, who'd introduced me in the first place—but given the dangerous territory I was venturing into, I didn't want to involve her.

Janet had been my best friend at USC. We'd met our first semester at a poker game, where I'd been dragged by a classmate from Stanford. He'd just started at the law school, and we went to the apartment of a couple of other first-years—where, he promised, the stakes were high, the liquor flowed, and a cute girl named Sylvia would be mixing cocktails. I wasn't much of a poker player, and was uncomfortable around all those grunting alpha types, but I immediately liked Janet—a college friend of one of the law school guys, and the only woman playing. She dealt and grinned slyly, occasionally raising her beer in my direction like I was in on a secret. In the end, she outplayed the guys, took the cash, and went home with the girl—Sylvia, the architect, with whom she now lived in San Francisco. After that night, I ditched my college friend in favor of Janet. She was the one grad student I could stand to hang out with, my other constant besides Chloe—and now, like Chloe, she too was gone.

The next Tuesday, at Mrs. W—'s house, I returned to her journals with new purpose. As I slogged my way through the monotonous pages, I started to read about some of the happenings I'd seen in the clippings—the parties that were mentioned in the paper, her early years with her husband. But there was little mention of her grandfather. Even if there had been, I wasn't sure it would be much help. The truth was, her prose was dull. Because this was her life, the only life she knew, she didn't see it as extraordinary; she couldn't place it in any context. She didn't accord it the wonder that other people did. But even if her writing had been the most engaging in the world, it was clear it wouldn't get me what I needed—something that would convince Professor Rose that there was fresh new information about Langley W— and the origins of the city. I needed to find out if her father or grandfather had left papers themselves—and I needed a way to get to them.

The written accounts were no substitute, either, for the woman herself. Each day, after I had finished my work, she'd invite me to join her for iced tea or lemonade—sometimes, when it was warm enough, out on the patio; sometimes in one of the sitting rooms, where she'd show me some new abstract sculpture or painting she'd bought, whose meaning I couldn't surmise. By this point she'd taken me to see more of the house—the various living rooms, each with a chandelier and fireplace; the wood-paneled library; the theater room with a full screen and large stuffed chairs; the laundry room with five industrial-strength washing machines. There were bars built into nooks after every few rooms, in case you needed a drink on your travels. This was a place built for parties, though the guests were all gone—if they'd ever been there at all. Now it was like a museum, a remnant of a different age. I didn't know how Mrs. W— made the decision of where to sit each day—but she did, and I followed her lead. Although she was always dressed in some impeccable outfit—she didn't seem to believe in casual—she'd sit with one of the dogs on her lap and ask how far I'd gotten that day. Then she'd offer commentary more interesting than what I'd just seen on the page.

"That Cecil Biscott," she began, about the man from whom she'd purchased a huge real estate holding in the South Bay, "he was married to the biggest slut in Beverly Hills, and he was so busy trying to keep other men's hands from up her skirt that his business fell apart."

Or, about an overdemanding artist whose show she sponsored at the museum: "He wanted a separate truck to ship each of his individual pieces, including one petrified tree stump he called 'The Root of the World.' I could have pulled a better stump out of my own back-yard. Can you believe it? I wasn't going to pay for that turd."

Or, about a gentleman who'd courted her after her husband died: "He wanted me to see him exclusively, but I wasn't going to commit. Remember: multiple choice is always better."

On Thursday, during my last visit for that week, it was just warm enough to sit outside. I finally ventured the nerve to ask, "Mrs. W—, when I'm finished typing your journals, are you going to make them available to the public?"

She looked at me as if I'd suggested cutting the dogs up to eat with our crackers. "Make them available? Why, of course not. We'll have them printed and bound to keep here at the house, in case my children ever care to learn about their mother."

"That's all? They'll just be for the family?"

She placed her teacup down with a violent clank, and I couldn't tell if she was caught off guard or angry. "That is plenty. And it's in keeping with how my family has always done things. My father's letters to my mother are bound and boxed in this house. My grandfather kept only a few of his papers—although some of his friends at the Colonial Club did put together a collection of re-membrances. You'll see, as you get further along, that I do write more about his life and accomplishments. But that is all for the benefit of my children and grandchil-dren. It isn't meant to be part of the public record."

"Well, that's a shame, don't you think?" I glanced at Mrs. W— and then looked out at the canyon, where a red-tailed hawk flew across our line of vision, harassed by a small, persistent bird. "I mean, your family has been integral to the formation of the city. But the Dohenys and Chandlers and Otises have gotten all the credit. It's like you said a couple of weeks ago—more people should know *your* story."

Mrs. W— shook her head and shifted in her chair, enough that the dog jumped off her lap. "We have never been the sort to self-aggrandize. Even when I sold my grandfather's business, people were surprised by the extent of our holdings. They had no idea we were so immensely rich."

This was true. The news accounts of the sale were breathless; it was one of the largest transactions ever involving a privately held company—an enterprise whose size and scope had previously been obscured.

"Why did you decide to sell?" I asked.

She hesitated; I knew I was taking a risk by pushing her. "The time was right; the demand for oil was so great." Now she emitted a disgusted huff. "Besides, oil is not a business for women."

I let this sit, half-curious and half-amused. Whatever Mrs. W— thought of oil, she certainly hadn't shied away from business.

"But having a written record of your family wouldn't be self-aggrandizing," I argued. "It would be filling in a crucial part of our city's history. If you don't mind my saying so, I think it would be hugely valuable."

Mrs. W— was quiet for so long I wasn't sure she'd heard this last part. But finally she asked, "And why are you so interested, young man?"

I worked to keep my voice steady. "I'm an historian.

This is an untold story. And I'd enjoy seeing your family's contributions get the recognition they deserve."

I realized my mistake when Mrs. W— boomed, "Recognition! All the people who matter in this city know who the W—s are!" But the storm passed quickly and she resumed her normal voice. "I don't trust anyone, Richard, to have our best interest at heart. That's why I no longer have events at the house, or even many visitors. People don't come to see me, you know, unless they want something."

I didn't know what to say to this; right then, it hit a bit too close to home. Finally Mrs. W— said, "I'll think about it." Then she sighed and looked as weary as I'd ever seen her. "At least *you* show some interest. That's more than I can say for my children."

Her children. Through all of our conversations over iced tea and lunch, she rarely mentioned them. Nor did they appear much in her journals. Looking ahead, I'd seen that her writings slowed dramatically after her third child was born and were sparse for the next two decades. Even when she started writing regularly again, there were few passing references to them. *I bought the beach house the year Bart turned twelve*, she wrote at one point. And: *Jessica married a complete nitwit and gave me idiotic grandchildren*. But she didn't, either in conversation or in the pages of her journal, speak of their personalities or what they were doing; I didn't even know where they lived.

I asked Lourdes about this one rainy afternoon when Mrs. W— was out. I had brought back an empty juice glass into one of the kitchens and found her unloading groceries, still wearing her yellow slicker. Lourdes was cordial but always a bit reserved with me—she'd probably seen her share of overeager young men, walkers spending time with Mrs. W— for their own entertainment, not giving much in return. But I was determined to keep working on her. After we'd exchanged casual references about our plans for the President's Day weekend— she, her husband, and their young daughter were going to Griffith Park after Sunday Mass—I asked, "Do Mrs. W—'s children ever come to visit?"

Lourdes gave an almost imperceptible shake of the head. She looked toward the window, where water was running in rivulets down the glass. Lourdes was a consummate household staffer and never aired her own opinions. But maybe the bad weather had gotten to her. "Mrs. Jessica and Mr. Steven, they only contact Mrs. W— when they need money," she said.

I let that sink in for a moment. "Where do they live?"

"Mr. Steven—he's the youngest—lives up in Carmel. Mrs. Jessica and her husband live in Santa Barbara with their children, in Mrs. W—'s other house. Mr. Bart, the oldest, he lives on a ranch outside of Bakersfield. He's different—he comes to visit sometimes."

"Do they call?"

Lourdes allowed herself what sounded like a disapproving grunt. "Well, maybe for Mother's Day. But not Mr. Steven anymore. He and his mother haven't spoken since the accident."

"The accident?"

Now something shut down in Lourdes's face and she turned toward the food she was unpacking. She brushed raindrops off a milk carton, a package of spinach. "I shouldn't have mentioned it," she said. "But it was bad, very bad. Mr. Steven was hurt. Others too."

"What happened?"

She was silent for a moment. Then: "I don't want to say any more. You shouldn't ask Mrs. W— about it. She'll talk about the children if she wants to, I suppose."

I stood staring at her, waiting for her to say something else, but she was finished; she placed the last of the groceries into the refrigerator, took her raincoat off, and left the room without another word. Finally I turned and went back to the office.

What rifts had occurred between Mrs. W— and her children? What was the accident? And why would Mrs. W— not want to speak to her son now? Certainly I could see that Mrs. W— could be difficult, but not visiting at all? That seemed a bit extreme to me.

Yet who was I to judge? It had been months since I'd seen my own parents, and they were just a few miles away, in Westchester. I'd avoided them out of simple embarrassment—there was no progress to report in terms of my schoolwork, and the paralysis was inexplicable. Why see them if all I could tell them was no, the dissertation isn't finished, not even close; no, I'm not teaching or doing anything else that might be filling my time, no, this certainly does not bode well for my future prospects in academia or anywhere else for that matter. Even when my brother called, saying my father needed cheering up because the business was struggling, I'd said no, I was busy, I couldn't. There was absolutely nothing I could do to help anyway, and I didn't need to make that more plain.

Maybe Mrs. W—'s children were similarly embarrassed—I'd seen no reference to any of them accomplishing anything of note. The only things I'd found were the daughter's wedding notice and the article about the youngest son being caught with the questionable woman. It had to be hard to be the offspring of the rich and successful. The second and third generations paling in comparison to the first, whose grit and mettle were diluted through the years. That is something that the children of the wealthy and the children of immigrants actually had in common, I suppose.

I finished up a bit of work—an account of a dinner party with then–Governor Reagan in Santa Ynez—and closed down the laptop for the day. By the time I went out to my car, the rain had stopped. The air still felt unsettled, though, and as I drove off the grounds and wound my way through the hills, huge, dramatic clouds lingered over the city, their bottoms lit pink from the setting sun. Out over the ocean, concentrated rays of light shot through the clouds and hit the water, illuminating bits of blue in the churning black. The sun lit up parts of the city too, highlighting neighborhoods and trees that looked washed clean. Toward Palos Verdes gray streams trailed from the billowing clouds; there, they were still getting rain. I pulled over to the side of the road to gaze out at the show. A stormy sky is so much lovelier than a clear one.

CHAPTER FOUR

The next week, I accompanied Mrs. W— to a lunch at the Polo Lounge. I'd never been inside the Beverly Hills Hotel, had only driven by on Sunset, but I'd always been amused by its pink-layered extravagance, which made me think of a birthday cake. Dalton pulled the car into the driveway and up to the front entrance, where a dozen blond bellhops in pink polo shirts and white pants all jumped to action like a flock of busy birds. One of them held the door open for Mrs. W— and guided her to the walkway, where she exchanged his elbow for mine and the two of us went into the lobby. It was marvelously overdone—green and pink everywhere, with stuffed chairs and love seats circling a planter that sprouted birds of paradise. Men strolled by in white hats and floral-print shirts. We passed a woman with teased-out curls and huge dark glasses, wearing a cream-colored coat with a fur collar. She was carrying a tiny dog of the same hue; I looked twice to make sure the dog wasn't part of the collar. I had on the second of the outfits from my shopping excursion—the trousers, jacket, and tie—and Mrs. W— was dressed in a cashmere turtleneck sweater and pants of gray material so fine it looked like it had been woven from clouds.

We made our way across the lobby, around the corner, and into the dark-green space of the Polo Lounge, passing a black-and-white photo of the hotel from 1912, when it was the only structure in the area. There was garden seating, but Mrs. W— preferred to stay out of the sun, and so we took a booth in the corner that gave us a view of the rest of the room. Across from us, in the opposite corner, was the wood-paneled bar, where even now, at eleven thirty a.m., men in jackets and ties drank martinis and sidecars. We were meeting the head fundraiser for a children's hospital, a place where Mrs. W—'s father had contributed significantly. She herself, she said, had made the mistake of giving a gift a decade before. We sat there for ten minutes, and then fifteen, and I took the time to look around, noticing the tall mirrors spaced every few feet apart—built, I suppose, so the famous clientele could surreptitiously examine themselves without having to leave their seats. With the velvet-backed booths, the decor, the piano, I felt like I'd wandered into a scene from 1952. All that was missing were the cigars. Finally, a nervous-looking, paunchy, middle-aged man with an alarming shock of dark hair approached the table, hand extended.

"Mrs. W—!" he said too enthusiastically.

She took his hand, not standing, and shrank back from his aborted attempt to kiss her cheek. "You're late," she said.

He looked so comically hangdog that I feared he might cry. "I'm, I'm sorry, Mrs. W—. I apologize. Traffic on Sunset was awful."

"It's always awful. You should have allowed for it. We did, didn't we, Richard?" I was caught off guard and didn't reply, but she kept talking: "Please seat yourself, Mr. Hathaway."

After an awkward bit of shuffling, he slid in next to Mrs. W— in the semicircular booth. "I'm Tim Hathaway." He reached out to shake my hand.

"This is Richard," said Mrs. W— before I could speak. "He's here to make sure you don't try to pull anything funny on me."

He looked confused for a moment, and then laughed. "Ah, yes! I'd forgotten about your wonderful sense of humor!"

Hathaway took a deep breath, visibly trying to settle himself down. He was dressed in a blue suit that was slightly too large, and I wondered if my own clothes looked incongruous on me; if my common background was evident despite the new expensive threads. When Hathaway talked, which he did nervously, earnestly, he'd pause dramatically for effect; twice, Mrs. W— turned and gave me an obvious look.

A black-suited waiter came over to take our order, and Hathaway resumed talking. He was filling her in on the happenings at the hospital—the new wing they'd completed, some research that was being done in conjunction with USC. He mentioned that the president, Dr. Cheryl Clarkson, had been at a press conference with the county supervisor that day. Mrs. W— interrupted.

"Is that why Dr. Clarkson isn't here?"

Hathaway was out of sync now; it was like a needle had been picked up from a record player and he didn't know where to put it down again. "She . . . excuse me. She had to meet with the county supervisors."

"Usually, when an organization wants something from me, the director comes to meet with me personally," said Mrs. W—. "She must not really want my support if she sent the second string."

A bit of color came up in Hathaway's cheeks and he seemed to shrink three inches. "It's no measure of how much the hospital values your support," he explained, "that you're seeing me today and not Dr. Clarkson. If we were making a solicitation, then of course she'd be the one here to meet with you." He paused, recovering. "But we're not asking you for anything today, Mrs. W—. This is strictly an *informative* lunch. To let you know, as we let *all* of our major donors know, about the latest happenings at the hospital."

"Well, if that's the case," she said, "you could have just sent me a newsletter."

Just then our lunches arrived—three McCarthy salads, served in amphitheater-shaped bowls. We turned our attention to the food—the bacon, chicken, cheese, and beets tossed with greens right there at the table. Mrs. W— must have gotten her point across, or perhaps she was just bored; whatever the reason, she let Hathaway chatter on about all the wonderful things at the hospital. I watched him—talking, gesturing, flashing an odd smile midsentence before his thought was complete; doing everything, in fact, besides performing backflips—and knew that there must have been dozens of him, hundreds, people and organizations who wanted something from Mrs. W—; who did everything they could to make her notice. For a moment I actually felt bad for Mrs. W—. How could you trust what anyone said when they were all trying to get you to give money? No wonder she didn't tell people when she did something good.

I ate about half the salad, barely tracking the conversation, sneaking glances at the other tables. The woman with the cream-colored coat and elaborate hair sat in one corner; I suddenly realized she was a vaguely familiar starlet. She still held her dog, which was more discernable now that she'd taken off her coat, and fed it little scraps from the table. The starlet was as thin and lanky as a baby giraffe; her dark glasses, with their coaster-like lenses, had the effect of drawing the attention she was pretending to avoid. Everyone worked studiously not to notice her; I think the only one who really didn't was Mrs. W—.

After our plates were collected and coffee was on its way, I excused myself to go to the restroom. The hallway was lined with photographs, old black-and-white pictures of young couples at the hotel pool, men in their tennis whites, all taken in the twenties and thirties. There were the predictable photos of Clark Gable, Bette Davis, Lana Turner, and others. I pushed my way into the men's room and found the nicest facilities I'd ever seen, wooden doors on the stalls all the way up to the ceiling, framed paintings illuminated with display lights above the urinals, and marble counters with cloth hand towels embroidered with BHH. There was also hair gel, razors, little bars of deodorant, even tiny samples of cologne. I pressed the dispenser on a ceramic bottle that I thought held soap, but it appeared to be mouthwash instead. After rinsing off the minty substance and finding the real soap—a small fresh bar for every person—I used one of the towels and deposited it in a wicker basket next to the counter. For a moment I thought about taking one to keep as a souvenir, but I suppressed the urge and went back out into the hallway.

As I made my way through the lobby and toward the Polo Lounge, a voice called, "Richard? Richard Nagano?"

I turned and saw Fiona Morgan, flanked by two other women. My heart jumped at the sight of her. I'd been thinking about her ever since the night at the museum, and it took me a moment to realize that she was really here—that I hadn't imagined her. She wore a blue sheath dress that clung to her figure, and carried a silvery purse that sparkled with jewels. The women on either side of her were dull in the face of her radiance. I took a step in their direction, and Fiona came toward me, gliding, as if her feet did not tread on the ground. Her carriage was perfect, and I remembered what Mrs. W— had said, that Fiona had been a dancer. Everything else in the room seemed muted, leaden, mere backdrop to her elegance.

"Hello," I said. I tried to control my face but felt it break into a grin.

"Hello! I was wondering when I'd see you again!" She leaned close and I wasn't sure of the proper protocol. A hug? A kiss on the cheek? She placed a hand on my shoulder and, holding her body away, turned her face toward my cheek for a sideways kiss. I don't think her lips actually touched my skin; it was more like a mutual cheek rub.

"Are you here with Mrs. W—?" she asked.

"Yes, she has a lunch meeting with some fundraiser from the children's hospital."

"Is it a middle-aged guy with too much hair? Tim Hathaway?"

"Yes."

"Oh, poor man. We deal with him too, for my family

foundation. He means well but he's no match for her. I'm sure she makes his testicles shrivel."

"Yes, I think I actually heard them," I said. A passing hotel staffer gave us a disapproving look, which Fiona ignored.

"Did you drive with her? Because if not, I'd ask you to join us for lunch. Or at least a drink. I'm with a couple of girls who are planning a fundraiser for a children's charity. Foster care," she whispered, as if it were a dirty term. She turned toward her friends and they waved at us, offering pinched, uncomfortable smiles. Now she leaned in close. "They're a bore, to tell you the truth, but I've got to do it, you know? They'd be totally lost without me."

"I'm sure you must be very helpful."

"Well, helpful or bossy. But in this case bossy may be helpful. These particular girls can't cross the street without asking their husbands."

In the daylight, she looked different, her skin paler, light freckles visible on her arms and shoulders. Her eyes were pale blue, I saw, and her hair a more complex blond, shot through with a bit of honey that might have been caused by the sun. Her features looked thin and almost severe, except for the full red lips; her bare shoulders were bony and I wanted to cover them, cup my hands over her skin. I still couldn't tell if she was pretty or just put together nicely. But I could not get enough of looking at her.

"It's nice running into you," I said, "but I need to get back to Mrs. W—. No telling what Hathaway has done to her while I've been gone."

"Or what she's done to *him*," Fiona said. Then: "You

always get pulled away just as we're starting to talk. How will I ever get to know you?"

I shrugged. "I'm a busy man."

"I know. You're working for Marion, plus you have your dissertation. I've been thinking about that ever since we met."

"Really?"

"Really. I told you, I think it's fascinating. What I didn't have a chance to mention, before we were interrupted by that awful Bryson Rutherford, is that my family foundation has been leading an effort to support alternative-financing mechanisms for minority-owned businesses. We're especially interested in the areas of East LA and South LA. We've looked at creating incentives for more favorable bank loans, but banks aren't biting, so we're trying to figure out what else might work. Your example of the Japanese prefectural association was really intriguing, and I'd love to hear more about it." Now she rested her hand on my arm, just above the wrist; her movements were controlled and graceful. "Would you like to have lunch with me sometime?"

Her touch sent a jolt through my body and paralyzed my tongue. "I'd love to," I said finally, trying to sound casual. "When?"

"How about a week from next Monday? At the Colonial Club? Twelve thirty?"

"Sounds good." I had no idea what the Colonial Club was, though I remembered Mrs. W— had mentioned it.

"Perfect! I look forward to it! It'll be great to spend some time together, just the two of us." She squeezed my arm and leaned in close again. "I want to know everything about you."

* * *

After Mrs. W— had sent Hathaway off with his tail between his legs, Dalton drove us back to the house. I hadn't done any work on the manuscript that day, so I went into the study while she retired for her afternoon rest. I noticed a book on the desktop that hadn't been there before, bound in fine brown leather. *Memories of Langley W—* was embossed on the spine and front cover. Pulse quickening, I opened the cover. The same words were repeated on the title page, followed by, *Recollections of his friends.* The book was published by the Colonial Club—where I was set to meet Fiona—in 1948. On the bottom, written in ink: *Copy 1 of 20.*

I closed the book and placed it back on the desk. My heart was beating madly. Mrs. W— must have left it here for me to read. She was trusting me with the only known personal accounts of her grandfather. What would I find here? Would some key to the family's wealth, to the history of the city, be hidden within? And most pressingly and selfishly, was there anything here that I could use to show Professor Rose that I had access to the W—'s papers?

A quick perusal convinced me that this volume—despite its obvious intrigue—would not work for my immediate purposes. My head spun at the identities of the contributors—two other city fathers who'd made their fortunes in oil, the then-president of USC, the head of the US Geological Survey, three mayors of Los Angeles, and several men whose names I didn't recognize, who appeared to be fellow club members.

I started to read a few of the contributions, but they were mostly second- or thirdhand accounts, and it was hard to believe the stories were true. There was a tale, related by the head of the USGS, of Langley camping out in the field during a survey in Colorado and encountering a bison. *Langley faced down the big beast, staring him right in the eye from no more than twenty paces: and lo and behold, the animal grunted, turned, and wandered away. He knew he was no match for old Langley!* There were accounts of his fishing expeditions at Yosemite and Shasta, with descriptions of hard-fighting rainbow trout that made them sound roughly the size of dolphins. There was a story of Langley single-handedly dragging a two hundred–pound drill bit from a truck to a drill site—and then dragging the old, broken, three hundred–pound drill bit out. There were descriptions of his generosity—from the founding of a school for orphaned boys, to his work with the Red Cross for soldiers returning from the World Wars, to his buying cords of wood for every family in his New Hampshire hometown during a particularly cold winter, to his assistance to an old friend from the early oil days, a man who'd helped him engineer a pipeline, who was destitute and blind in his later years. *It occurred to me that I didn't sufficiently compensate you for your work at the time,* he was quoted as saying. *And so I have decided now to provide you with back pay.* There were several accounts of his funeral, which was held at the First Congregational Church. Amongst the tributes and decorations had been a ten-foot replica of an oil derrick made entirely of flowers. So many mourners turned out for the service that the church had to close its gates.

These all seemed like affectionate but overblown portrayals, fellow men of influence who nostalgically inflated the memory of one of their own. There was nothing here I could easily lift, no convincing event; it would be far too risky to commandeer the whole book, and I was afraid even to take a picture with my phone in that too-dark room, as if the book's fine paper—and even its leather cover—would disintegrate if exposed to a flash. So I placed it on the top left corner of the desk and tried to think of something else.

I pulled the most recent volume I'd been working from off the bookcase, but glancing through it, I knew it wouldn't give me what I needed. It was nearing desperation time—I was due to meet Professor Rose on Tuesday, and this was Thursday. What could I possibly find? Then something occurred to me. The volumes I'd been working on chronicled Mrs. W—'s early adulthood; she was already nearly twenty when they started. But Janet had typed up the pages from the earlier volumes, the ones I hadn't looked at. When Mrs. W— was younger, when she was a girl, her grandfather still alive.

I picked up one of the two earlier volumes that lay on a lower shelf. The notebook was leather-bound like the rest, but smaller, to fit a child's hand. I carefully opened the front cover and found the words *Marion W—: Her Life and Times* written in ornate childish cursive on the front page. On the next page, her account began: *I was born in Los Angeles in 1936, into the happy home of Robert and Helen W—. Robert is the only son of Langley Stuart W—, one of the most important men in California.*

My heart jumped. Even though this was nothing earth-shattering, just the mention of Langley made me hopeful that I'd find something good. Yet the first few pages were again disappointing. There was a lengthy description of their house in Hancock Park and of the meals prepared by their cook. She referred to her parents as *Father* and *Mother*. It appeared that Father was often away, and even when he was home, he was usually offstage. Father was in his study while her big brother Langley opened presents on his tenth birthday. Father took a telephone call while the family sat at dinner. If he was there, it was as a looming or slightly threatening presence: *Father was cross at Mother for taking us to the beach without his permission. He did not want us playing in the sand like common urchins.*

About thirty pages in, the story took a turn, when young Marion, her big brother, and her parents moved in with her grandparents while the new estate in Bel Air was being built for her family. They were staying at the family home off Sunset, the ten-thousand-square-foot mansion on four secluded acres that I'd read about in my earlier research. This sounded like a happier time. The narrative described Easter egg hunts and games of hide-and-seek as well as a two-room treehouse. There were three dogs—two Brittany spaniels and a German shorthaired pointer—four cats, a pair of peacocks. There was a stocked fishing pond where Marion would sit for hours, listening to the songs of birds. And central to all of these stories was the figure of Grandpa Langley, the self-proclaimed Captain of Mischief. He took Marion fishing, he taught her how to climb a tree, he would jump out from behind corners during hide-and-seek and hold Marion tight and tickle her. He'd appear in the bedroom where she and little Langley had been confined for misbehaving, and smuggle in bowls of ice cream. In all of these accounts, her grandparents, and especially Langley, were described as boisterous and happy. Her father was a void of silence.

Things changed when Marion's grandfather departed sometime in late summer, for an extended trip to Mexico for business. Since her parents' new house was still under construction, they stayed on at her grandparents' home. Without Langley in the narrative, the pages grew dull again. There were accounts of a visit to a new school for her brother, of a long and silent family dinner. I leaned back in my chair and tilted the book up so I could read it from this inclined position.

Then I turned another page and something slid out and hit the desk. It was a postcard. From the blank space on the page and the dark marks on the corners, it was clear that it had been glued to the paper. But time had loosened the adhesive and released the card, which I picked up cautiously and read.

Baby girl bear, it started. And as I read on, the card seemed to come alive in my hand:

I'm so sorry to miss Thanksgiving with you. Business isn't half as fun as fishing with you and Langley, but I do it for you, do you know that? I hope you eat double your usual amount of turkey, cranberries, and stuffing. Grandma loves to see you both eat. Where I am, the little boys and girls are so skinny and sad. Not rosy and round-cheeked like my babies. I hope you have a wonderful Thanksgiving Day. And if Papa Bear is grumpy again, tell him to go sleep in his den. I'll be home in two more weeks, by Christmas for sure, and then we will play and play.

With love and a big warm furry embrace,
Grandpa Grizzly (aka Langley the Furriest Bear)

I turned the card over and looked at the front: a faded color drawing of the Zócalo in Mexico City. Then I turned it back over to the written side. It had been addressed to *Ms. Marion J. W*—, at the address I recognized from my reading. The date was November 2, 1946. Mrs. W— had been ten years old.

I slowly lowered the postcard back onto the book and pressed my hands to my head. My heart was pounding wildly; I couldn't believe my luck. This was a postcard in Langley W—'s hand. Dated, stamped, and sent to Marion W—, and at his own address. And it was loose, separated from the notebook. I leaned to my right, pulled my own hardbound notebook out of my shoulder bag, and placed it on the desk. I looked out the window again, swung around in my chair to make sure the door was closed. Then I picked the postcard up and slipped it into my notebook.

Three days later, in Professor Rose's office, I sat on the Throne of Pain and cut right to the chase. I placed the hardbound notebook on her desk, opened it, and pulled out the postcard, which I had since put into a protective plastic sleeve. Then I turned the postcard around so that the writing was facing Professor Rose and slowly pushed it across the desk.

Professor Rose leaned over and looked at it—silent, curious, intent. Her red hair, which wasn't tied back today, hung loose on either side of her face. Her brow furrowed, then smoothed again; her lips opened slightly. Then she carefully picked the card up within its plastic sleeve and turned it over to peer at the front. Finally she placed it back down and looked up at me. Her eyes were animated, though I couldn't read her expression.

"This is . . ." she began. "This is extraordinary."

I almost collapsed with relief. For the last three days I had hardly slept, afraid that a fire or earthquake or theft would divest me of my quarry. Afraid that Mrs. W— would realize the card was missing, or that Professor Rose would not believe it was real. "It is something, isn't it?" I said.

"Up to now, I figured that nothing written by Langley W— survived. It was thought that his widow burned his papers."

"Not all of them."

"Well, maybe not *any* of them. Who knows? The family's always been so private, it would be just like them to say that things are gone when they aren't." She smiled now, and her cheeks were flushed. I had never seen her quite this worked up. Maybe it was the nerdy glee that all historians feel over previously undiscovered material. Or maybe she was thinking of her own ambitions.

"There's more where that came from," I said.

She pushed the card back toward me, as if afraid to be responsible for it—or as if she didn't trust herself not to take it. "What's your theory about him?" she asked.

I was caught off guard. "What?"

"What's your theory about Langley W—? What will your thesis be? I'm wondering what the key to his success was—how he found the oil. Did he bribe the government? Turn a geologist to his side? Take advantage of Native lands?" She leaned forward so far I thought she might grab me by the collar. "And where are the bodies buried?"

"I—" I wasn't sure how to address this. "I'm not

quite at that point yet, to tell you the truth. I've just now gotten access to these other materials. I'm sorry, Professor Rose, it's just early. For today, I was only trying to establish that I do have access to primary sources."

She leaned back and put her hands up. "Of course, of course. I don't want you to rush to conclusions when you haven't had a chance to review the materials. Urgency is no excuse for sloppy scholarship. But yes, this is more than enough to prove to me that you have access. Thank you, Rick. I'm very excited about your project!"

"Me too," I said, trying to sound more enthused than I felt. My immediate concern was different. "So, would this be enough to make you feel comfortable writing the letter for the fellowship renewal?"

Professor Rose looked at me as if she'd forgotten all about the fellowship and its relevance to my immediate life. "Of course, of course, I'm sorry. I'll definitely write the letter. I do want you to continue being supported. This possibility, this project . . . it could really be something remarkable."

After agreeing on next steps—I'd have to write a summary of the materials I found within a month, and formulate a thesis by May—I slid the postcard back into my notebook, put the notebook in my bag, and got out of there. I was giddy as I drove back home. I'd have funding for another year; I wouldn't be out on the street. And Professor Rose was on my side again. This was all cause for celebration—as long as I didn't think too hard about what I'd just done—and so as soon as I got home, I decided to go get a drink. It was just after five, when people were leaving their offices and school, released into the rest of their lives. But whom could I

call? Janet, the most logical choice, was gone; she'd texted several pictures of herself, looking happy, in front of
San Francisco landmarks. There were a couple of other
students from my dissertation support group, but they
weren't really friends—and besides, I couldn't tell any
of them what had saved my ass with Professor Rose. I
could go next door and grab a beer with Kevin, but he
wouldn't understand the reason for my joy; he was a
practical, in-the-world guy, a cowboy paramedic with a
physician's-assistant girlfriend, and the study of history
was esoteric and irrelevant to him, removed from the
everyday work of helping other people, not to mention
the task of making a living.

With a pang I thought of Chloe, the evenings we'd
spend having drinks and nachos during happy hour at
the closest Mexican restaurant. She would have been
happy for me, or at least relieved. Suddenly I missed
her with an intensity that cut through the general mal-
aise and loneliness I'd felt since her departure. What an
ass I'd been. When we first started dating, I'd conde-
scendingly treated her studies at a teacher credentialing
program as somehow less important than mine. She was
preparing to be a third-grade teacher; I was engaged in
serious scholarship. But somehow she'd gone from that
program to actually teaching third grade, to continuing
on to an administrative credential, to now serving as
a vice principal for an elementary school in Crenshaw.
The next principal position that opened up would probably be hers. And here I was, still in graduate school,
still playing around with history. No wonder she'd lost
patience with me.

I didn't really feel like staying home. So I put on another outfit Mrs. W— had bought me—a Tom Ford jacket-and-pants combo from my second appointment with Rafael—and went back out to my car. There was a place on Beverly that I'd driven past a couple of weeks earlier—one of those high-end gastropubs that had sprung up all over the city. I didn't go to these kinds of spots very often—the twelve-dollar burgers and eight-dollar beers had put me off—but now, with a wallet full of cash and fancy new threads, it seemed as good a time as any to do so.

I parked in a spot around the block, forgoing valet, since the Honda would negate the effect of the clothes. Through the windows, the place looked lively, crowded, bright, and for a second I felt a surge of doubt. But I pushed my way in, and was hit by a wall of sound. Everyone was talking, laughing, all in loud voices. Something metallic and alternative was playing over the sound system, and the flat-screens over the bar had the Lakers game on. "Welcome to Beer Lab!" chimed the two identical-looking blondes behind the front desk. Then they seemed to say in unison: "Would you like to sit at one of the group tables, or wait for a more intimate one?"

There were large, rectangular communal tables that held ten or twelve people, surrounded by smaller two- and four-person tables. All were filled with loud-talking people in their twenties and thirties, with plates full of huge burgers and fries, and pints of blond or amber or earth-colored beer.

"Can I just sit at the bar?" I asked.

"Sure!" the blondes said, and then one of them led me to the only empty seat. The barkeep was a nondescript middle-aged, block-headed guy with a beard maybe a centimeter long; I thought I recognized him from a recent commercial for something embarrassing, laxatives or erectile dysfunction.

He handed me a single-sheet menu printed on light cardboard and said, "Let me know when you're ready."

I looked at the selection of beers—all Beer Lab varieties—and the food items, the salads and nachos and fried calamari. The house burger here was fourteen dollars. Still, I was hungry, so I ordered a burger and an IPA.

I glanced around, trying to be subtle. To the right of me was a couple in their thirties, talking about the commercial real estate market. To the left were three young women who seemed to work together at a talent agency; they complained about a bad-tempered boss and a particularly difficult client. The brunette of this threesome made eye contact with me and I smiled. Looking at them, in their blouses and simple skirts, I felt a bit overdressed. Most of the guys were in button-down shirts, with just a few wearing jackets. But better overdressed than underdressed, I thought, as I took a swig from the beer the barkeep had placed before me. And I was proven right when the brunette from the talent agency said, "Is anyone joining you? Or are you here by yourself?"

I turned toward her, trying to give her a knowing, sophisticated smile. "I'm all on my own," I said.

"Well, *that's* a shame," the girl replied. "Or maybe not. Not for me, anyway."

She wasn't unattractive, not at all, and now she slipped past her friend, who moved over a seat, and placed herself right next to me. When she stood, I saw that she had a nice figure, more curvy than the usual self-starving Westside girl.

"Well, what brings you here all by yourself?" she asked, looking directly in my eyes, making her intentions clear. For a moment the image of Fiona Morgan flashed before me, her elegance and height, the skin of her shoulder. But I shook it off—tonight I was in this bar, with this woman, whose bare knee now pressed against my thigh.

"I just finished a business meeting and needed a drink," I said. "I'm a lawyer in Century City."

CHAPTER FIVE

The next Monday, I met Fiona Morgan for lunch at the Colonial Club. I'd learned, from the Internet, that it was one of the original private clubs in Los Angeles, a bastion of the city's elite. Langley W— was a member in the early 1900s, and it had been exclusively male for more than a hundred years. It had only admitted women for the last two decades, and Mrs. W—, not surprisingly, had been one of the first. Rumor was it still wasn't welcoming to Jews or people of color—there were references to lawsuits and protests, as well as conflicts with the state, which at one point had prohibited public officials from holding business meetings there. Reading all of this, I wondered how I would be received.

I arrived at the Colonial Club just after noon. I'd been so worried about finding it that I'd allowed too much time, and now, to save the embarrassment of being there so early, I circled the block a couple of times and then returned and pulled into the driveway at twelve twenty. Although I went downtown frequently to do research at the public library, or eat in Little Tokyo, or see exhibits at the art museums, I had never noticed the Colonial Club. Now I wondered how I'd overlooked it. It was an anomaly of ivy-covered brick walls and stone windows and doorways, like what I imagined East Coast establishments to be, as if a building had been plucked from nineteenth-century Boston and placed, incongruously, on the streets of modern LA. When I pulled into the garage—which was off the street and around a corner, to shield the members' comings and goings—I surrendered my car with a pang of self-consciousness and told the attendant I was the guest of Ms. Morgan.

"Who?"

"Fiona Morgan," I said, fearing I was in the wrong place.

"Oh, Mrs. Aaron Morgan," he said, and then ushered me into the front entrance, where an older black gentleman in a full crimson suit and white gloves gave me a once-over and said, with a slightly disapproving air, "Mrs. Morgan is waiting for you in the fifth-floor dining room."

The decor of the front entrance was expensive and old-fashioned—heavy furniture, floral rugs, and paintings of pastoral scenes. The elderly gentleman guided me to a small elevator and deposited me inside, repeating, "Fifth-floor dining room," as the heavy doors drew shut. My heart was beating nearly out of my chest—not only because I was about to see Fiona, but because I felt like an interloper who'd wandered onto royal grounds, who might be discovered and escorted out at any time. When the door opened, I walked out into more plushness. In front of me was a giant oil painting of a mountain region, maybe somewhere in the Sierra. On the table beneath it was an iron statue of a cowboy on a horse, corralling a bull. To the left there was a sitting area, where several men in their sixties wearing jackets and ties were gathered around low wood tables. To the right was the dining room—a huge, high-ceilinged,

wood-paneled space with square tables arranged diago-
nally all the way to the end. There must have been fifty
or sixty of them, as well as more tables tucked in nooks
along the windows. They were covered with plain white
tablecloths and utensils I didn't need to be told were
real silver. About half of the tables were occupied, all by
people older than my parents. I was the youngest person
in sight, and the only one who wasn't white—except for
the servers, who were all black and Latino, and who
moved gracefully among the tables holding platters.
Again, I felt like I had walked into a scene from another
era—an excursion not just through class, but through
time. An older gentleman—the maître d'?—approached
and asked if I was there for Mrs. Morgan. When I said I
was—how did he know, did I look that out of place?—he
led me to her table, about two-thirds of the way back
on the right side. Along the walls were more paintings
of mountains. I recognized, at one table, an LA city
councilman, and at another, a prominent philanthropist
whose picture appeared regularly in the paper.

"Richard! Hello, darling!" Fiona called out as we
approached. She stood for a cheek-kiss greeting, which
I proffered more smoothly this time, and I took in the
form-fitting light-blue suit she wore, the softness of the
fabric. I felt self-conscious in my own clothes—the same
jacket I'd worn to the Polo Lounge, but a cheap pair of
slacks, and a tie I'd bought that morning at Nordstrom.
Most of the clothes that Mrs. W— had bought me were
at the dry cleaners, but I'd needed to fancy up to meet
the dress code.

"You look lovely," I said, and then regretted it. Was
this out of line?

"Oh, please," Fiona responded, "I look like hell. I just dug this suit out of my closet because I couldn't fit into anything else. I've gained a few pounds with all of these luncheons."

"That's hard to believe," I said as I took my seat. "You seem very fit."

"Well, thank you. It's not easy being a woman, you know. We have to work so much harder for our beauty."

We were seated, not across from each other, but on either side of a corner, so that as I moved my right arm and she moved her left—I hadn't realized she was left-handed—our hands touched. I felt a jolt run through me; there was more heat in this one chaste touch than in all the sweaty acrobatics with the girl from the talent agency. I was sitting alone with Fiona Morgan, in a place that felt as unreal and inaccessible to me as King Arthur's court, and I had not the first clue of how to conduct myself. But this void was filled by Fiona, who immediately started talking about a benefit she'd been to the night before, her friends' struggles to choose the right schools for their children, the meeting she had scheduled for later that afternoon with the director of the Music Center. I only caught about half of what she was saying, partly because I knew so little about the topics she addressed, partly because I was mesmerized by her presence. Her blond hair was again pulled away from her face and gathered into a perfect bun; everything about her appearance was glamorous, untouchable. When she smiled—which she did often—she revealed perfect white teeth; when she threw her head back in laughter, I admired the lines of her neck.

A waiter appeared with a bottle of white wine; he

was wearing a dark jacket with a white pin affixed to it. He looked about the age of my father, and he smiled at Fiona and gave a respectful nod.

"Hello, Ricardo!" she enthused in return. "Meet another Ricardo—my friend Richard Nagano."

"Hello," I said, thrilled to be called her friend. Was I supposed to shake his hand?

But he kept his distance and nodded politely and said, "Welcome to the Colonial Club."

"Get whatever you want, Richard," Fiona said. "Everything's delicious."

I hadn't really had a chance to look at the menu, and now I was filled with anxiety. Everything sounded extravagant. Chilled poached salmon on a bed of organic greens. Filet mignon with a red wine pepper sauce and mushroom risotto. And no prices were listed anywhere. Fiona may have sensed my hesitation, because now she said, "Go ahead. You're my guest."

I tried to protest but she'd have none of it, and so I ordered pasta primavera—it seemed the least expensive— while she asked for the salad with salmon. After the waiter filled both our glasses generously with sauvignon blanc, she said, "Tell me, Ricardo, what does your pin mean?"

The man looked uncomfortable, shifted under the platter he held. "We're trying to unionize, miss," he said quietly.

Fiona had been leaning in, and now she frowned. I wondered whether she'd come out with flat disapproval or a polite word of noncommitment. Instead, she straightened up and said, "Good for you! It's about time these bastards paid you properly." When he shuffled off looking relieved, she added, to me, "I hope they ream this place."

I laughed, surprised, not sure how to react.

"You think I'm kidding? These guys need to be paid a living wage. Running around after all of us and keeping all our secrets."

"Well, I agree. I'm just surprised. Your sentiment is so—"

"Liberal? I know. My family can't stand it. As you can imagine, I come from a long line of Republicans."

"So how did you end up . . ." I wasn't sure how to complete the thought, "feeling differently?" I somehow overlooked the fact that she herself was one of those bastards; she and her family were longtime members.

"I just opened my eyes and started noticing things," she explained. "But my parents, they thought they'd done something wrong in raising me when I started paying attention to issues of inequality. They went through deep grief when I told them I was voting for a Democrat. I think they would have had an easier time if I'd told them I was a lesbian."

"Were you?"

"No. Well, briefly. In college." She grinned and took a sip of her wine and I laughed with her, not sure what to say. Then she leaned closer and looked into my eyes. "I've been doing all the talking. Now it's your turn. So tell me, what's your story?"

"Oh, I don't really have much of a story."

"We all have a story, whether we share it or not. Where did you grow up? Where's your family?"

I felt a twinge of self-consciousness, followed by guilt. "I grew up in Westchester. My dad's an electrician, just like my grandfather. My dad's office is on Jefferson, near Crenshaw. My mother works in a pharmacy."

"Really!" said Fiona, with an enthusiasm that seemed out of proportion to what I'd said. "Did your family used to live in Crenshaw?"

"Yes, my grandparents had a house there, and then my parents did too, until my brother and I were school age. Then they moved us to Westchester, for the schools." Ah, Westchester: the not-quite-Westside. Near the beach, so people could boast that they lived by the water. Yet no one would mistake Westchester for Santa Monica or the Palisades. For one thing, it was racially mixed—the escape hatch for blacks and Japanese who'd come from grittier areas. It was also so close to the airport that when planes took off, you could read the fine print on their bellies.

"Well, *that* makes sense," Fiona said, straightening up. "The schools in Crenshaw are just awful. There are a couple of decent charter schools now. We support the Inner City Education Foundation, mostly because Mayor Riordan did, and my mother does whatever he says. But there couldn't have been much of anything when you were growing up." She took a large sip of the wine that Ricardo had just poured. "We send a group of fifth-graders from South LA to summer camp each year. They go for two weeks to this lovely camp in Malibu, where they fish, ride horses, and go on nature walks. Sometimes I drive out to watch their final culmination. It always breaks my heart that they have to go back to South LA."

I didn't point out that I'd spent part of my childhood in South LA, or that I lived there now.

"And where did you go to college?" she asked.

"Stanford. Class of 2001."

"Really!" And now she looked at me in a different way. "Well, you're younger than me, not surprisingly. I was Wellesley, class of '96."

"Really?" I said, genuinely surprised. "You must have graduated when you were, what, fourteen?"

She laughed. "You flatter me, Richard. Really. I'm several years older than you."

"I don't believe it." It *was* hard to believe. "And where did you go to high school?"

"Marlborough. Of course. Like my mother. And her mother. And hers. When you were at Stanford, did you know Parker Ludlow or Christian Wade? I think they might have been in the same class."

"No, they don't sound familiar."

"Well, I suppose they wouldn't. They were probably off drinking and playing golf all the time. They wouldn't have graduated—or gotten in, for that matter—if they hadn't been legacies. And neither of them has accomplished anything since, unless you count massive summer parties in the Hamptons and Europe and a couple of stints in rehab." She took another sip of her wine. "But we're getting off track here. So your father's an electrician, and your grandfather was an electrician—were they just thrilled that you got into Stanford?"

"Well, yes. But my parents . . . it's hard for them to understand why I'm still in school. They'll be happy when I get a real job. My brother's been working with my father for years, and he'll take over the business when my father retires." That was, I thought, but didn't say, provided there was still a business to take over.

"And yet your dissertation is related to your family's business, right?"

I paused for a moment and drank some wine. Which dissertation should I talk about? The one I'd just proposed to Professor Rose? Or the one I was actually working on? "Yes, exactly."

"How far into it are you?"

"Oh," I said, embarrassed, "it's coming along. It's just that, since I'm not teaching anymore, I'm living off a fellowship, which is great, but not quite enough. That's why I took the job with Mrs. W—."

"How long is the fellowship?"

"Hopefully through next year. I'm not sure, though, if it's going to be renewed."

"Do you want me to talk to the president?"

"The president?" I looked at her blankly. "Of the Blain Foundation?"

"No, silly. Of USC. He's a good family friend. He'll make sure your funding's extended if I ask him."

"Oh. No. But thank you," I stammered. "I'm sure I'll find out soon."

"Anyway, tell me more. You said your work centers on the revolving group credit mechanism that provided the early capital for your family's business."

With the prospect of someone actually being interested in my topic, I probably told her far too much. I told her of my grandfather's joining the Okayama kenjinkai in 1928, the monthly picnics and excursions to the beach or the mountains, Tuesday bowling nights. I told her of him meeting my grandmother at a coffee shop in Crenshaw, and how her father was one of the original contributors to the revolving fund. I told her of my grandfather opening his business, and how he could only find work amongst other Japanese, and later the African Americans who moved into Crenshaw, but never the whites. I told her of how, when my grandparents were sent off to the internment camp during the war, their black neighbors kept watch over their house and business; and how my family's loyalty to their clientele had made them keep the business in Crenshaw, even when their rising income and the changing racial tides would have allowed a move to a fancier area. I told her of the other loans the kenjinkai made possible—to the Japanese language school, to several gardening ventures, to a nursery, even a funeral home. And I told her of how the members pooled their money too, to help families of members who'd died.

Through all of this, Fiona looked at me attentively, seriously, as if hearing about the workings of a different country, which in some sense I suppose it was. "It's a lovely concept," she said.

Our lunches arrived, on china plates with decorative flowers. I released the silverware from the napkin; it looked too fine to dirty with food. And then Fiona told me more about what her foundation was trying to do: team up with a few other family foundations to create a pool of capital for small businesses in the inner city. Some of the major banks had promised loans to minority businesses, she said, but then set the credit expectations prohibitively high. As she spoke, she'd put some food on her fork and hold it above her plate, then raise it to her mouth, and lower it again, never putting it in. She would do this three or four times with each forkful, and I watched first with interest and then growing frustration as the fork made circles in the air, since I didn't want to eat unless she did. Finally I decided I had to go ahead—I was starving—and tried not to be too distracted by her.

"*Our* idea" she continued, waving a forkful of greens, "is that *any* business owner would qualify as long as there was proper collateral." She smiled and took another sip of wine. "So what do you think?"

What did I think? I thought it sounded well-meaning but completely naïve. Honest people like my father would never trust someone like her or take what they perceived as a handout. And dishonest people—and there were plenty of those—would fleece these people blind. But I wanted to keep her talking, and smiling, so what I said was, "That's a very interesting idea."

I felt a twinge of guilt now, thinking about my father. Growing up, I'd rarely seen him in daylight. By the time I'd wake up at six fifteen, he was already gone for the day, driving to his office off Crenshaw before he headed out to job sites. After he and his crew finished their work for the day—at a house, an apartment complex, an office building, or hotel—he'd go back to the office, where he'd return messages, process invoices, and order supplies before coming home for the evening. It was almost always dark when he turned into our driveway. My mother would sit with him while he ate dinner, a warmed-up version of whatever she'd made for my brother and me that night, after her own shift at the pharmacy was over. She'd always held the family together. My mother was from Polish stock, dark-haired and gray-eyed, and in pictures of my parents from the early days of their courtship, they're good-looking and fresh, a mixed-race couple in a time when such unions weren't common. If there was any protest to their marriage on either side, I never heard about it. My mother would have shut it down anyway.

I didn't talk much with my father those evenings. After he ate, he would settle into his recliner and watch his beloved Dodgers, sometimes followed by the late-night news. By the time he'd settled in, I was already in my room for the night—doing homework, or talking on the phone, dreaming of the world beyond Westchester. When I wandered out to the kitchen to get a drink, he'd wave at me wearily. And on Sundays, his one day at home, the only time I saw him in daylight, he'd smile at my brother and me, delighted, surprised, as if he couldn't quite believe that he'd made us.

Suddenly I felt a large, hostile presence at the table; I looked up to see the unpleasant man from the museum event. He was wearing a blue jacket with some kind of insignia; he looked like an overgrown frat boy.

"Fiona," he said gruffly, with an irritated edge to his voice.

"Oh, hello, Bryson," she said, smiling up at him brightly. "You remember my friend Richard Nagano."

"Sure. You're the artist," he said definitively, in a way that allowed no room for correction. He didn't offer his hand, and neither did I.

"You weren't at the Performing Arts Center dinner last night," he said accusatorily, as if she'd stood him up for a date.

"I had another event," Fiona replied, still smiling. "For John Thomas Dye. Fanny Halstead was the committee chair, so I really wanted to support her. Otherwise I wouldn't have missed it."

"Your husband was there," Bryson thrust at her, and this struck home. She blushed—was she surprised?—but regained her composure quickly. When she looked up at him this time, though, her smile was different, tighter.

"Aaron's very invested in the center's success, you know. Especially since his company did the initial design."

"That's why I was surprised you weren't there."

"Well," she rejoined, and now her smile was radiant again, "now that I know that *you* were, I'm glad I stayed away!"

A red flush crept up Bryson's face, and once again, I got the sense of violence barely contained. "Have a nice lunch with your friend, Fiona. Maybe we'll see you at the Country Club."

When he was gone, Fiona downed the rest of her glass in a single gulp.

"Who *is* that guy?" I asked. "What an asshole!"

"Keep your voice down," Fiona said, but she was giggling, and she covered my hand with her own. "And pour me more wine." When I complied, she took another sip and then told me about Bryson Rutherford. He was the heir to a major insurance magnate from the early twentieth century. He had a beautiful but quiet wife, whom I'd met at the museum, and two large but meek sons.

"What does he do?" I asked.

"He plays golf."

"No, I mean for work."

"So do I."

I paused, letting this sink in. I understood she didn't mean professionally. "He's rather aggressive with you," I remarked.

"Yes. He wants to sleep with me."

"Really? He has a funny way of showing it."

"That's how it is with so many of these men," she said. "They're used to steamrolling everyone to get what they want, and they're befuddled when someone resists."

"Is your husband like that too?" I ventured. The wine had given me courage.

"No," she said wistfully. "My husband is a gem. A good father. Commanding and assertive at work, of course, but kind with his family. It's a pity I don't appreciate him more." She was quiet for a moment, then looked up brightly, clearly finished with the subject. "Mrs. W— knows Bryson's family well. Her grandmother was a cousin of Bryson's uncle on his father's side."

I tried to untangle this in my mind but quickly gave up. "She's never mentioned him," I said.

"She wouldn't. He's a tool. And she has too much of a sense of decorum to talk about anything unpleasant."

I wasn't sure this was actually true—she talked plenty about unpleasant things, and people she didn't approve of. But I didn't push it. I was learning that Fiona spoke often with absolute certainty regarding things she knew nothing about.

"How do you like working for her?"

"It's fine," I said. "It's interesting."

"What are you doing, exactly?"

I was hesitant to answer, but decided it wasn't giving too much away. "I'm typing up some papers for her—old documents that were written in longhand."

"Really!" Fiona exclaimed, with a bit too much interest. "Family documents?" She cocked her head slightly. "She must really trust you."

"I guess so."

"She hasn't always had it easy, you know," Fiona said thoughtfully. "I mean, she's always been rich. But she lost her husband young—in her thirties—and never remarried. And her brother died when she was a teenager. It's strange—people call them overdoses or accidents now. Back then you knew what it really was—a suicide."

"That must have been tough on her."

"I imagine, but you'd never know—she's always carried herself like nothing touches her. Probably something she learned from that father of hers, who was apparently a real bastard."

"Was he? She always speaks so fondly of him."

"Yes, I know. But from what my parents say, he was terrible to do business with, and drove his wife to drinking. He'd leave Marion all alone in that big mansion of theirs while he went off on trips, and was mean to her when he was around. He was nothing like his father, and maybe he knew it. Everyone thought the world of Langley. Everyone."

I didn't know how to react to this. Nothing was as simple as it seemed. Mrs. W— had all of life's advantages, and yet they hadn't shielded her from heartbreak.

"She's got this hard shell," Fiona continued. "But then she surprises you. You've heard her talk about undocumented immigrants, right? Or as she calls them, *illegals*."

"I have, yes."

"She pretends to be so hard-line, but you know her housekeeper Maria?"

"Yes."

"Well, Maria used to work for Donovan and Carly Ford."

"Donovan Ford . . . the guy who ran for the state assembly maybe five, six years ago?"

"Yes, he's a son of Beverly Hills who's on a bunch of boards and was also a city councilman. Well, it came out that he and Carly had some undocumented immigrants on their household staff, and he's a Republican, you know, and it wouldn't stand."

"So . . ."

"So they made a big fuss of being surprised, and of publicly saying they would report their staff to immigration officials—including Maria, it turned out. Then Marion W— stepped in and hired Maria away, and she must have pulled some other strings too, because—as you see—Maria was never deported."

"But how did Mrs. W— do that, and why?"

Fiona shrugged. "Who knows? The Fords entertained a lot, and maybe Marion came across Maria and was impressed with her. Or maybe she just wanted to stick it to the Fords—she never liked Donovan."

"Wow." I didn't know how else to reply.

"You work out of her house?"

"Yes, and what a place! It's like an oasis up there. I can't believe it's part of the city."

"I know," Fiona said. "I've been there. Marion used to host the most spectacular parties—beautiful black-tie affairs, with live music and dancing, waiters balancing trays of drinks through the crowd. They were magnificent, like how you'd imagine parties in the 1920s. It was tradition mixed with modern style. Like Mrs. W— herself, I suppose."

"It's hard to imagine a party up there. The house is totally empty except for her and her servants."

"How often do you go?"

"Three times a week."

"And she never has visitors?"

"Not that I've seen."

"Not even her children?"

I snorted. "*Especially* not her children. Her assistant said they never come to visit. Except for the oldest one, sometimes. Bart."

"Bart," Fiona said, making a sound between a scoff and a sigh. "Nice guy, but a bit of a bumpkin. He lives somewhere in the Central Valley."

"So I heard."

"He runs a cattle operation. And he's really into it. He's not just a gentleman rancher. He does a cattle run every spring and fall, takes his herd up into the mountains for summer grazing, and then back down again. It's rather quaint. I mean, have you ever heard of such a thing?"

Actually, it sounded pretty cool to me, but I didn't say so to Fiona.

"Does she talk about them?" she asked now, pointedly.

"What? Who?"

"Her children. Does she talk about them much?"

"No, she's hardly mentioned them."

This seemed to satisfy Fiona somehow. "It's strange, no one sees them anymore," she said, looking away. "Especially since Steven's accident."

"What happened with that anyway?" I asked cautiously. "No one will tell me anything. Not just about that—about any of Mrs. W—'s kids."

Fiona drew back, her face taking on a serious expression I couldn't quite read. It didn't occur to me to wonder why she'd had so many questions. I had too many questions myself. "It was terrible," she said, leaning forward again. "Really tragic." She paused, and in the silence I heard the din of voices, a hundred of Los Angeles's wealthiest people enjoying their lunches, far above the streets of the city. "Have you heard of Cliffhaven?"

"Cliffhaven . . . I'm not sure."

"It's a big estate up along the Central Coast. About twenty thousand acres. It's the property of the Larson family down here in LA. Ben Larson founded Larson Oil around the same time that Langley W— got started. Their family is richer than God."

I nodded. If someone of Fiona's set referred to a family as richer than God, then their wealth must have been unimaginable.

"Anyway, the original mansion's mostly closed now, just used for special events, but there's still a large house on the property, and an airstrip. This generation's Larson, Charles, spent a lot of time there with his family and friends. He didn't have to work—he just managed the family money—and he would go up there with his friends and their families to drink. Well, two years ago they were there for Steven's fortieth birthday party, and someone got it into their head that they wanted to see how fast Charles's Porsche would go. So all these men— these grown, drunk men—got into Charles's car—with his twelve-year-old son!—and drove it high speed down the landing strip. No one knows quite what happened, but the car went over a cliff past the end of the runway. Later they said that the skid marks suggested it was going well over a hundred. At any rate, Charles was thrown and killed, and so was his little boy. Another man was terribly hurt. And Steven—he survived, but he broke his collarbone, his leg, and several ribs. Somehow he made it out of the wreckage and crawled back to the house. I hear he'll limp the rest of his life."

"Jesus."

"I know. What a waste. Charles's poor wife and daughter are still a mess to this day. And I have no idea how the other man is doing."

I shook my head, immediately understanding why Mrs. W— didn't speak of this. "Did Steven come home to recuperate?" I asked.

Fiona shook her head. "No. He was in a hospital in Santa Barbara for several months, but Mrs. W— wouldn't see him. People said she was furious—she couldn't believe he'd been a part of something so tragic and stupid. She'd had to get him out of jams before, and she was probably tired of his misbehavior."

"That seems kind of harsh."

"Oh, I wouldn't feel too sorry for Steven. He's caused more than his fair share of damage."

We were both quiet for a moment as I tried to digest the story. "So who was the fourth person?" I asked. "The other survivor?"

"I'm not sure. He wasn't part of our circle." She paused. "It's *strange*, you know, that no one knows who he is." And now she leaned closer and put her hand on my wrist. The warmth of it, the slight caress she gave me with one finger, made it hard to focus on what she said next: "Like maybe there's more to the story."

"You could be right," I responded, trying to gather myself. "Was there ever anything in the paper?"

"The paper?"

"The *Los Angeles Times*. Or the *San Francisco Chronicle*. Or whatever paper they get up on the Central Coast."

Now Fiona sat up straight again and gave me an indulgent smile. "Oh, Richard. Nothing important ever gets into the paper."

After a strong cup of coffee, which I needed to counteract the wine, I left Fiona, who stayed behind to speak with a group of delighted older men who were bent over a game of backgammon. I made my way back down to the garage and tried to pay the head valet, but he shook his head and said, "Mrs. Morgan has paid. And our drivers do not accept tips."

I put my money away, embarrassed, and stood in the waiting area with several men in business suits and an elegantly dressed older couple. The woman wore a jacket and skirt that seemed too heavy for the season, dark glasses, and expensive-looking jewelry. I was so caught up in staring at them that I didn't notice that my Honda had already arrived and had apparently been sitting there for some time.

"Ma'am? Is this your car?" one of the valets asked the older woman.

Her eyebrows furrowed in displeasure. "Certainly not!"

CHAPTER SIX

I n the top drawer of my desk, in a cheap manila folder, I keep a collection of invitations and programs—from the openings, parties, luncheons, and dinners I attended in the months I worked for Mrs. W—. There is a rectangular menu, printed on thick card stock, from a luncheon in a private home, detailing in blue, engraved ink the progression of courses: charred kumquat salad, roasted Hancock Farms quail with black garlic miso, triple-chocolate miniature cake with bourbon-raspberry garnish. There are square, embossed invitations—works of art themselves—to charity functions or galas at the Beverly Wilshire, the Ludlow, and the Beverly Hills Hotel, which never include a printed address because, of course, such information wasn't needed. There were printed price sheets for pieces at art exhibits—no item less than $50,000—as well as glossy programs for high-end fashion shows, at which the world's top designers revealed their designs for the new season.

I remember with a touch of disbelief some of the more extravagant moments of these events—the dinner where Omar Santiago, the famous designer, auctioned off a week on his private island in the Caribbean, complete with a concert by Placido Domingo; the time that François De-Lorme, the French celebrity chef whose restaurants dot the Westside, arranged to cook for a wealthy bidder and his twenty closest friends in the winner's private home. And the evening at Tiffany's on Rodeo Drive, where tall, sinewy models slithered around the store showcasing pieces of jewelry, each of which cost more than the current model of my car.

The people who attended these gatherings were people I had only read about in magazines. There was Betty Baker, whose family owned all the Baker department stores. There were descendants of the founders of Beverly Hills. There were several Delaneys, of Delaney Steel, a couple of Hearsts, and members of the Price and Jameson families. Carly Ransom, the granddaughter of the founder of Perennial Pictures, was part of this set, as was Hattie Clark, whose father had founded Clark Pacific Railways. Being around them was like rubbing shoulders with history. There were a few families of more recent vintage too—Mr. and Mrs. Hal Westbrook, of Westbrook Aviation; Ben Laughlin, the head of Bluestone Wealth Management, now in jail for securities fraud. The Mr. Ernest Bestharts, of Best Heart Builders, would sometimes attend, and Mr. Jay Calchinek, the head of Starlight Finance's California operations.

The one thing all these people had in common, of course, was wealth—wealth of the unimaginable variety; wealth that could only be whispered at; wealth that made them feel, to me, like members of a different species. And yet, as I learned, wealth alone did not earn membership in this exclusive group. The old historical families—those with roots in the late 1800s or early 1900s, or those whose families hailed from the East—were of the innermost circle. The next level out were the venture capitalists and their wives, who were tolerated but not embraced, privy only to the less exclusive events—because of the suspicions regarding how their fortunes had been obtained, or simply because they were, as Mrs. W— once sniffed, "new money." None of the tech millionaires ever attended these events— which were formal and square—and the dot-com kids were too young, anyway. And only on occasion would we see movie and television stars, because "street people," as Mrs. W— explained, "do not mix with show people." Strangely, the second- and third-generation heirs seemed to look down on people whose wealth was self-created. And it goes without saying that all of these recipients of inherited wealth were white.

Mrs. W— always drew attention at these events. People would come over to pay their respects, and she'd smile at them ironically and entertain their effusive greetings and then, often with a mildly cutting remark, send them on their way. I saw the fear in people's eyes as she approached; I saw them trip over themselves to be polite.

"What did you think of that speech?" one woman asked, about a powerful testimony at a charity function.

"Who cares?" countered Mrs. W—, yawning loudly. "I'm just here for the inedible lunch."

Or: "Here comes the insufferable Waverly Stone. Richard, do you have my antacid?"

Or, at a table that also included Cardinal McCloud from the archdiocese: "I'd consider attending church, you know. If the priests would stop buggering little boys."

Or, at a table of ladies so proper that they barely seemed to speak: "My grandfather was one of the first men to climb Mt. Whitney, you know. But if he did it now he'd have to carry out his own poo."

And yet people circled her, came to her, watched her from afar. She did not want them, and so they couldn't get enough of her. Or at least it seemed she didn't want them—I didn't think to ask why, if she found these people so tiresome, she continued to grace their events. But I understood why she needed accompaniment, for I served as her escort, her confidant, her bouncer. Me, the kid from Westchester, the son of an electrician. Me, the dapper mixed-race man, dressed in Canali suits that had been picked and purchased for me; by now I'd made several more trips to Rafael's store, and had a personal shopper at Neiman's. Mrs. W— would hold onto my arm, using me like a shield. And when she was ready, usually well before the event had come to a close, I would lead her through the crowd so she could leave.

At all of these events, always, was Fiona—giving air kisses to everyone she saw; throwing her head back in exuberant laughter; touching people lightly and complimenting their clothes; floating through the room like a perpetual hostess, or a politician trying to win votes. I thought of what she must have looked like in her dancing days, gliding gracefully across the stage. She was always dressed—as were all of the women—in spectacular clothes, form-fitted dresses and suits; the women would hold their heads up perfectly, profiles always visible, as if they knew they were going to be photographed. Which—thanks to the step-and-repeats, the photographers from society magazines—they almost always were. Fiona would pay her respects to Mrs. W—, and after their strange, almost wry exchange, she would throw her hands up happily and greet me. I wanted to believe that there was something there beyond her usual ebullience, some response that was reserved for me alone.

"My friend Sherry can't keep her eyes off you," she whispered thrillingly in my ear. "But I told her I found you first."

"You'll have to come say hello to my table," she said another time. "Though the girls might not ever let you leave."

These whispers would be accompanied by a touch on my hand or shoulder that felt more than just casual. I didn't know whether to believe in them, yet I enjoyed them anyway. After each of these events I'd return to my desk at Mrs. W—'s, or my couch at home, and lose myself in my imaginings of her.

I wanted to gain Fiona's attention, to be with her alone, but how? She didn't offer a second lunch invitation, and I knew it would be improper for me to suggest we meet again. I was at the mercy of the luncheon circuit, but those luncheons only afforded me a few moments with her in public company—no time for private conversation, for studying the finer points of her face. I kept remembering the feel of her hand cupped over mine at the Colonial Club, when we talked about Steven J—'s accident. She thought there might be more to the story. If I helped her figure it out, would she touch me like that again? I didn't know. But because I wished to please her, because I needed a place to focus my energy, and because my curiosity about Mrs. W— now extended beyond her notebooks, I decided to find out more about the accident. I wanted to figure out who the fourth passenger was, and why his name—and even the accident itself—was not in the public record. I told myself that this was no more questionable or intrusive than showing Langley W—'s postcard to Professor Rose.

So one afternoon, when I got home from a luncheon, I sought out Kevin. I found him at the back of our complex, working under the hood of his Ford Explorer, massive arms streaked with oil. Kevin's family had lived next door to my grandparents in Crenshaw, and he'd been my classmate at Westchester High, another South LA transplant whose parents had moved him for school. But he, like me, had never felt at home there; the old neighborhood had called him back. He was a football player, and after high school he'd been a linebacker for USC. Then he'd bounced around for a couple of years before getting a job as a paramedic, and now he was just a few months away from finishing his nursing degree. Kevin and I had stayed in touch through our families, and he and Rosanna had told Chloe and me when the apartment had opened up in their building. We'd all been friendly, and during that awkward period in which one couple figures out how to adjust to the other half being broken, both Kevin and Rosanna had watched out for me. They'd made sure I ate in those first lonely months, invited me over to watch ball games on the weekends, their laughter and banter in Spanish—hers fluent, his choppy but trying—a salve for my wounds.

Kevin had been urging me to get back out there. He'd also tried to set me up a couple of times, an offer I'd declined—and when he saw me standing there in my blue jacket and yellow tie, brogues shined to the point of reflecting, he stood up straight and whistled.

"Look at you, Mr. *GQ!* And where have *you* been this afternoon?"

Kevin was big—6'2"—and almost always cheerful, which had struck me as a strange temperament for a frontline paramedic. But maybe his good-naturedness was exactly what injured, maimed, and frightened patients needed in their moment of trauma. Or maybe he was just trying to stay sane.

"I had to go to a charity luncheon," I answered.

"Ohhh," he said, dragging out the syllable and standing delicately with his toes together, in imitation of a lady. "A *charity* luncheon. And since when has my starving grad-school buddy had the bucks for a charity luncheon? Or those threads you have on? I thought you were kind of a charity case yourself."

I paused, suddenly self-conscious. Even for dressy occasions, neither Kevin nor I had ever dressed like this. And only once had I seen my father in a suit, at my college graduation. I was so used to him in his workingman's clothes—the black pants and blue work shirt, with *American Electric* in yellow script across the pocket—that the sight of him in dress clothes had been startling. The gray suit fit him loosely, like he'd purchased it a size too big to take advantage of a sale. And he shifted in it uncomfortably, looking down at his cheap, unpolished shoes whenever someone greeted him. My father, who could create and uncouple mysterious electrical connections, could not converse with these fancier parents. He could not get past the first introductions. The other students' parents were doctors and financiers, attorneys and public officials; some of them did not work at all.

And yet here he was, and my mother too—who despite her simple clothing and Target-bought handbag did not believe she was lesser than anyone.

I remember feeling exposed somehow, like something essential and previously disguisable about me had suddenly come to light. I saw the curious looks in my classmates' eyes, the patronizing smile of a girl I was trying to flirt with. And seeing this, I felt a sinking sense of embarrassment. It didn't occur to me then how awkward and uncomfortable that weekend must have been for my parents, despite their pride in my accomplishments. It didn't occur to me that it was a burden for them to pay for two nights in a cheap hotel—nothing close to campus was affordable—and to miss two days of their jobs. All I was aware of was how they reflected on me.

"I went as someone's guest," I explained to Kevin now.

"The guest of some young lady, I presume."

I hadn't told Kevin much about my job—it was too strange and complicated. So he'd come to the conclusion that I was involved in a new, intriguing, slightly scandalous romance—which I let him believe, maybe because I wanted to believe it myself.

I tried to smile mysteriously. Then I brought up the business at hand. "So this young lady," I said. "She was telling me about a bad accident that happened a couple of years ago."

I gave him the broad outline of the accident up the coast, the deaths and the unknown fourth passenger. I told him I'd tried to find an account of it in the media, and had come up empty. By this time Kevin had walked around the front of his car and was leaning back against the driver's door, his muscular arms crossed and brow furrowed. With his light-brown skin, square jaw, and cool green eyes, he'd been a total lady magnet—not just for the many women who wanted to date him, but also for those who sought a protective big brother. He listened, engaged, as if my problem was his own.

"So you can't figure out who the fourth guy was?" he asked.

"It's not just him. It's the whole thing. I can't find *anything*—not even a record that the accident really happened."

"Are you sure it *did* happen?"

"I'm sure."

He didn't ask how, and I was grateful for that; Mrs. W—'s affairs, and Fiona's story, were more than I wanted to get into.

"My hunch is that the fourth guy is from some other powerful family," I continued, "and that they didn't want word of his involvement reported in the press."

Kevin nodded thoughtfully. "Could be."

"So . . ." I ventured, "do you think the hospital up there would have a record?"

Kevin shrugged his shoulders. "Who knows? There's nothing on the Central Coast itself, you know. And I'm not sure that San Luis Obispo has a trauma center."

I felt deflated. What had I been thinking, anyway? That a hospital would reveal confidential information about its patients?

"But one thing I'm pretty sure of," Kevin said now, "is that the paramedics would have been called. And I've got a buddy who works for the fire department up in SLO, and maybe he could look into it if I asked him."

My heart surged. "Really? Kev, that would be amazing."

He grinned. "Your girl will be pleased with you, huh?"

I blushed and didn't respond to this.

Kevin asked, "When did you say the accident was again?"

"I'm not sure, exactly. About two years ago. It was at a big estate, and there was an airstrip they drove off of, and two people died. The property owner and his son. There couldn't have been too many accidents like that."

Kevin slapped the car with his big right palm like a play had been called and he was ready to run it. "All right, I'll ring Chris. Bastard owes me anyway—I covered for him a few months ago when he came down here to see his secret lady. He's a fireman, and you know how it goes for them—he can't fight them off. He played right tackle for UCLA, but he's all right."

It didn't take Kevin long to get back to me. Two days after we'd talked in the carport, I came home from Mrs. W—'s to find a yellow Post-it stuck to my front door:

R—
Where are you, man? Text me when you're home.
—K

I did as instructed, and within two minutes there was a heavy knock that would have scared the hell out of me if I hadn't expected it.

"Jesus, Kev," I said, pulling the door open, "you don't need to knock it down."

"I can't help it if we live in a place with cheap-ass construction." He stopped short as soon as he'd made his way inside. The place was a mess. There were papers and books scattered across every flat surface, a couple of bags from El Pollo Loco and McDonald's, a greasy pizza box, which would have revealed, if he'd lifted the lid, one piece of days-old dough and colored material that had once been a slice of Supreme. The sad thing is that it actually looked better than it had four months ago, before I'd gone to work for Mrs. W——. But Kevin hadn't been inside, I realized, since Chloe, whose design flair, kitchen appliances, and general extreme neatness had made the small apartment feel homey.

"Uh, I guess your new girl hasn't been here yet."

I ignored this. "What did you find?"

Now Kevin met my eyes again, mess forgotten, and grinned—I knew, and he probably did too, that without Rosanna, his place would have looked much the same. As it was, he was at-home casual—tan cargo shorts and a yellow Lakers T-shirt with a conspicuous tear at the shoulder, a USC cap atop his head.

"My man Chris called me earlier," he said. "And he knew exactly what you were talking about. Big accident, fatalities, up at some rich people's spread on the coast. They had to speed up Highway 1 from SLO to get there."

My stomach catapulted up into my throat. "And the time frame sounds right? Two years ago?"

"Yeah, exactly. Chris remembered because he'd always wondered about the property and had never expected to see it. He said it was a weird scene—stupid-ass rich guys totally wasted, a bunch of women crying. The car crushed like a beer can, and all the passengers thrown. And then, he said, the accident wasn't reported. Usually so little happens up there that it's front-page news when an elephant seal makes it up to the road. But there was nothing on this accident on the news or in the paper. Nada."

I tried to keep my breathing steady and moved my messenger bag from one chair to another, to keep from looking at him so he wouldn't see my face. "And does he remember who was in the car?"

"He remembered the father and son who died—the Larsons, I think—because their family owned the property. But he didn't remember the others. Had to call his buddy in the ER at San Luis Obispo Hospital, and he remembered. Some dude named Steven J—."

"That's what I thought." It amazed me that this name, this son of a family that took up so much of my waking hours, should be totally unfamiliar to Kevin.

"And the other was a guy named Jimmy Castillo. He remembered 'cos one of his teammates, a lineman, was a Jamie Castillo."

I let this settle, let our voices be still and this name take life—gave it space to breathe in the room and in my mind, new and unexpected.

"You're sure?"

"I'm sure. Chris said so, and what he says, you can take it to the bank."

"Do you know what happened to them?"

Kevin shrugged. "I don't know, man. Chris never heard word of them again. He said both the guys who were still alive that night were messed up pretty bad. J— broke some bones—his legs, I think he said, and a bunch of ribs, some internal bleeding. The other guy was even worse. Had a head injury, and broke his back. Chris isn't sure that he even survived."

I'd moved over to the window now, my back to the room, and I felt Kevin looking at me. "Dude, what's this about?" he asked gently.

I tried to laugh, but it sounded strangled to me, and I'm not sure my nonchalance was convincing. "Just trying to figure something out for a friend," I said.

"That girl, right? She must be something else. I hope you know what you're doing, man. I hope she's worth it."

When Kevin left, I opened a beer and sat at the dining room table. The accident that his friend told him about was clearly *the* accident. But who was Jimmy Castillo? I'd assumed he was one of the men of Steven and Fiona's set, but the name threw me. Sure, there were a couple of Latino surnames among the people I'd met over the last few months—but they tended to be the married names of women who'd hooked up with rich Spaniards or Argentinians, or, in one case, the name of a wealthy white Cuban. And that first name: Jimmy. Maybe he was Spanish or Argentinian—or Chilean, or Cuban—too. He couldn't be Mexican. It just wasn't possible. There *were* no Mexicans, Chicanos, Central Americans, Puerto Ricans, or anyone else who could remotely be conceived of as brown, or black, or Asian, in Fiona's or Mrs. W—'s world. The only person of color was an ambiguous halfbreed: me.

I wanted to share the news with Fiona, of course. I wanted to tell her what I'd discovered and then accept her pleasure and gratitude—like a schoolboy who'd found a girl's lost, beloved kitten; like a kid bringing home a report card full of As. She had given me her cell phone number before we met for our lunch, but while I'd brought up her contact information on my phone several times, I'd never actually used it. Now I picked up my phone and tapped out a text: *It's Richard. I found out who the fourth person was.* For a moment I thought of typing Jimmy Castillo's name, but that felt too stark, too revealing—I had no idea where she was or who she was with. I set the phone back down on the coffee table, expecting a wait, but it buzzed almost immediately with her reply: *Can't talk now but the fundraising luncheon for the children's charity is tomorrow. Want to come? The Randall estate in Beverly Park. 11 a.m. XOXO*

And so, a little after ten a.m. the following day, I drove over to Sunset, turned into one of the canyons, and worked my way up the meandering streets of the Hollywood Hills. Mrs. W— had been invited to the luncheon too, but was feeling under the weather, and so— for the first time—I was attending alone. The massive estate was in a gated complex, a half-mile in from the guard station on Mulholland. A suited valet opened my door and kindly ignored the make and condition of my car as he wrote me up a claim ticket.

There was already a sea of ladies on the cobblestone outside of the enormous house—women mostly in their thirties and forties, dressed in lunchtime finery. I knew from Fiona that a few of them were in finance or law— members, she said, of the working class, by which she meant they had to work. Many of them wore floral patterns of pink, light blue, orange, or yellow. I swooned at the combined effect of pastels, perfume, and tinkling laughter. This group made the gatherers at the LACMA event look as casual as the crowd at Coachella.

A table was set up on one side of the driveway where six young women appeared to be checking people in. These were clearly staff—either of the household or, more likely, of the children's organization that was benefitting from the event. Unlike the champagne-sipping crew, several of these women were Latina, Asian, and black.

"Oh, you're a guest of Mrs. Morgan's," one of them said, finding a handwritten place card with my name on it. "Your table number's on the back."

"Where do I go until lunch?" I asked, though she was already on to the next guest.

I turned back to the crowd, which had swelled again; I'd learn later there were over three hundred people. Where was Fiona? I resisted the urge to text her. Without Mrs. W— as my cover, I was free-floating, unmoored; I felt totally invisible. There were a few other random men, unlucky husbands or boyfriends who were huddled together off to the side of the crowd, as if they were foreign bodies expelled from the main organism. I took a step in their direction before realizing that I'd have nothing to say to them. They were the Bryson Rutherfords of the world, the men of the leisure class. To those men—and in reality—I had more in common with the charity employees, or the staff. A server walked by with a tray of champagne glasses and I took one; maybe getting drunk would help me make it through.

Suddenly both halves of the front door opened, and the ladies poured in, like sheep rushing through the gates and to their pens. I hung back so as not to get crushed, drafting off of a group that moved less urgently.

Inside the house, a group of women were clustered around a small raised stage where four tall, almost inhumanly beautiful models stood mannequin-like, swiveling occasionally, their eyes trained above the heads of the crowd. Young men in tuxedos whisked through with platters of hors d'oeuvres—raw salmon in delicate pastry cones; asparagus wrapped with beef; tiny round quiches; miniature Chinese food boxes filled with a bite or two of noodle.

The front hall opened to what looked like three different living rooms, all decorated with plush furniture and a mix of tasteful but uninteresting art. Through one of the rooms and down the hallway, I heard someone say, was the ballroom. It was hard to imagine the kind of life that required a private ballroom.

"Is that where the lunch is?" I asked a cluster of ladies, who looked confused that I'd addressed them.

"Oh, no. It's a *spring* luncheon, dear," one of them said. "Spring luncheons are held *outdoors*."

I continued past the stage and outside, where a second structure sat behind the first, with one wall entirely open to the yard. Here, there were more long tables, which held items for a silent auction. There were one-of-a-kind handbags; there was a weekend in Napa at a luxury hotel, including a round-trip flight on a private jet; a diamond necklace whose first bid outpaced a year's worth of my rent; a trip for four to a castle in Scotland.

I turned back toward the main building and finally saw Fiona. She was wearing a bright red dress that clung inspiringly to her figure. Her sunglasses were dark, large, and round, Audrey Hepburn style; the jeweled watch on her wrist accentuated the fineness of her bones. My heart fluttered despite itself.

"Richard!" she cried out cheerfully, flinging her arms open, glass in hand, managing not to spill a drop of her drink. "I'm so glad you were able to come!"

She gave me a cheek-to-cheek air kiss and then introduced me to several women, two of whom I recognized from the Polo Lounge. "These are the ladies who did the *real* work," she said, in a way that made it clear that in fact they hadn't done much. "Our poor destitute children in the foster care system are so lucky to have them."

She kept her hand on my arm as she talked, and it felt like that was the only thing holding me in place. Her friends did not know what to say to me, and so they talked amongst themselves.

"Is that a Valentino?" one of them asked the other, noting her dress.

"No, Oscar de la Renta."

"Oh, it's lovely. Even better than the Nanette Lepore you wore last year."

"Well, *your* outfit is fabulous. Geoffrey Beene?"

"Yes. Don't tell anyone, but it's actually from a couple of seasons ago. I got it in '08 after the market crashed, when all the stores were marking things down."

"I remember how bad it was. I mean, the parking lot at Saks was almost empty!"

Fiona squeezed my arm and gave me a dazzling smile. "I have to sit with my friends at lunch, since I'm part of the host committee. I'm sorry. But please sit with me now, for the fashion show."

"The fashion show?"

"Yes, Le Farrier is debuting his fall collection here today. It's the talk of Beverly Hills. Can you believe it? That's why so much of the fashion press is here."

Not only could I believe it, I had no idea who Le Farrier was. The crowd was now moving again. I let Fiona guide me, hand still curled around my arm, through the second structure and out to another part of the property, which featured the loveliest swimming pool I'd ever seen. It was set in cream-colored marble, and the water was a dark cerulean blue; at one end was a terraced structure of stone, a kind of fountain that fed a steady stream of water into the pool. Laid across the entire length of the pool was a sleek black path, as thin as a carpet, that had been rolled out over the water. "That's the runway," whispered Fiona incredulously. At the other end of the pool was a line of shrubbery behind which the models must have been dressing; draped on the wall behind the terraced waterfall was a huge black banner with *LF* printed in silver. There were white, cushioned folding chairs lined up on either side of the pool, and we found seats about three rows back; directly across from us, in the front row, sat two former First Ladies. I mean, of the United States.

When all the ladies had taken seats, the music began—loud, pulsating beats from an invisible sound system. From behind the hedge emerged the first model, whom I recognized from the stage in the entry hall. It looked like sections of several unrelated dresses had been sewn together to create her outfit. She sashayed toward the pool and then—almost miraculously—onto it, gliding over the thin black walkway and above the blue as if walking on water. The crowd let out a collective

"Oooohh!"; I held my breath, expecting her to sink. But she didn't. Then a second model followed, in a pantsuit that looked slightly military. How did the runway hold them up? How did water not splash on their shoes? Were they so weightless that their presence didn't register?

It went on like this, models in elaborate, impractical clothes, walking back and forth across the pool, the thumping club music on a continuous loop. Next to me, Fiona and her friends dissected each outfit, deciding which ones might be considered for purchase, and which ones simply admired. I watched the First Ladies shade their eyes with the programs, which listed the names and prices of each outfit. I thought for a moment about taking a picture with my phone, but noticed that nobody else was taking pictures. Apparently the event was so commonplace that it did not require documentation.

Finally the show concluded, and all of the ladies clapped and cheered. Fiona leaned over and repeated her apology for not being able to sit with me at lunch; she suggested we meet afterward for a drink. Then she was off, moving in her effortless way, blending into the crowd.

I stepped out of my row and away from the pool, approaching a tall brunette who was standing back from the others, observing her surroundings.

"That was quite something," the woman remarked, smiling. "Have you ever been to a fashion show?"

"No. This is my first."

In her simple white suit, this woman seemed a little underdressed for the occasion. And yet there was a sense of ease about her, a kindness in her eyes, that immediately made me feel less out of place.

"Are you enjoying the event?" she asked.

I paused. "I've never felt more at home."

Now she laughed out loud, with real delight. "It's over the top, I know," she said. "But it's the only way to shake any money out of these ladies. And I do care about this organization. My husband and I have two foster kids ourselves. Once you have any experience with these kids and that system, no amount of giving is enough." She looked troubled for a moment, and then the smile was back. "I'm Caroline Randall, by the way."

I racked my brain wondering why this name sounded familiar. And then I realized—the Randall estate. This woman was the hostess.

"I'm . . . Richard Nagano," I stammered, embarrassed by my earlier sarcasm. "I . . . I work for Marion W—."

"I know. Good to meet you, Richard." She offered her hand for shaking. "I'm so glad that Marion found you. She pretends to be such a hard case, you know, but she's nicer than you think."

"I'm learning that," I said. "And thank you, ma'am, for having me today."

"Oh, please, don't call me *ma'am*. It's Caroline. Now let's get to the best part of this party: the food."

I followed Mrs. Randall down the stone walkway and into yet another yard. This new space was spotted here and there with huge, beautiful old-growth trees; it had once been, she told me, a park. Set between the trees were dozens of round tables, as well as a small raised stage, all of this framed by an expansive view of the San Fernando Valley, the San Gabriel Mountains beyond.

My handwritten place card indicated that I'd be at table 27, which turned out to be so far off to the side that it was almost in the bushes. When I made my way over, there was only one spot left, between a forty-ish too-thin society blonde and a normal-seeming woman of thirty or so, who worked for the charity. There was a printed menu on heavy card stock, and from that I learned that the meal—and hors d'oeuvres—had been prepared by the famous French chef François DeLorme. In addition to his restaurants, he'd created a line of products that took up entire sections of Whole Foods, and his cable TV show was one of Chloe's favorite diversions. Mrs. W— ate at his restaurants often; for a moment I wished she were there. The preset salad, with farm-to-table ingredients, was the best I'd ever had; the crusty, rosemary-tinged bread was like heaven. And I was glad for the culinary distraction, because the anorexic blonde—whose name was Alexa—could not stop complaining about the terrible view from our table, when it was clear that what really bothered her was being seated with miscellaneous unattached guests and employees of the charity. It could not have helped that the charity staffer, a perfectly pleasant young woman named Sarah, was lovelier in her natural, unaltered state than most of these fancier ladies.

There were speeches—by Caroline Randall, who gave the greeting; by the head of the event committee; by a B-list actress. They described the children served by the charity beneficiary: kids in abject poverty, kids shuffled between multiple foster homes; horrid accounts of abuse. I realized with a jolt that the actress was *genuine*; she'd been a foster child too, she said, and had endured unspeakable treatment. As she spoke, her voice wavered a couple of times, and I found myself quite moved. Yet throughout her speech, which included a story of her brother being burned with cigarettes, I heard the clink of silverware on plates and the continuing buzz of voices, saw waiters dipping down to place or pick up dishes. No one was paying attention.

I made small talk with my tablemates and savored my fish—arctic char so tender it might have just been pulled from an Alaskan stream. But when one of the speakers shifted from describing families who lived off of less than $15,000 a year to announcing winning auction bids of twice that much, I had to step away. There was a break in the hedge right near us, through which servers had been moving silently with trays. I excused myself and slipped through.

I felt something of the relief of having escaped a burning house; now, standing outside, I could breathe. Here, away from the tables of ladies, servers whisked back and forth from yet another building on the property, where the food was being prepared. I glanced at the activity and then simply stared at the building, trying to gather myself. Maybe the path around the side of the building led out to the street. Maybe I could continue past it and leave.

"Quite an event, isn't it?"

I looked up and saw that the person speaking to me was none other than François DeLorme. He was slightly shorter than me, smaller than he looked on TV, with windblown gray-black hair. He was wearing gray pants and his ubiquitous chef's smock. I couldn't speak for several seconds, but finally eked out some words.

"Yes, it's . . . the food is delicious." For all the A- and B-list stars I'd seen in the months I'd worked for Mrs.

W—, all the members of important families, this was my first moment of being truly awed, acting like a tongue-tied fan. I kind of admired this guy—he had come from a humble background to achieve worldwide fame; he'd gone from a rural village in France to a mansion in Holmby Hills. And it was true, his food was delicious.

"Thank you," he said, and then I realized that this wasn't what he'd meant; he hadn't been fishing for compliments. "I've lived in Beverly Hills for more than twenty years," he said, "and these spectacles never cease to amaze me."

"Yes, these ladies are something." He'd immediately pegged me as not belonging. Was it that obvious? "But some of them are nice."

"They're awful," he said.

I didn't know how to respond to this, and so we stood silently for a minute, watching servers go by with trays of plates full of half-eaten fish, expensive food that went straight to the dumpster. It occurred to me that the famous chef's smock was quite dirty, smudged with food stains, and I realized that he didn't just leave the cooking to minions, that he still did the actual work.

"Well, I think . . . these ladies are lucky to have you. They must know that. I mean, you're *famous*. More famous than all of them put together."

"Caroline Randall is always respectful to me and my staff, that is true. The rest of them are not."

"I can't believe that."

The chef laughed. "Young man, let me tell you a story. That second woman who spoke, the head of the events committee? She and her husband are regular customers of my first restaurant in Brentwood. They come in at least once a week, and sometimes my wife and I have a drink with them after dinner."

A server walked by with a plate of desserts, and the chef stopped him, readjusted a mint leaf on a slice of cake, and then sent him on.

"Well, last month I was visiting my new restaurant in Paris. It was packed; it had only been open for a couple of weeks—this is my first restaurant in my home country, you see. That same man and his wife are there, on their annual vacation to France. Only I didn't know they were coming and was delighted to see them. I have a bottle of champagne sent to their table, gratis, because it's busy and they are having to wait. But when I go over to say hello, you know what he does?"

"What?"

"He looks at me, and in front of everyone, in my home country, he says, *Where's my fucking food?*"

The luncheon broke up a half an hour later and I finally made my escape. I texted Fiona and let her know that I would be in the bar of the Pinnacle Hotel, a couple of miles down the hill off Sunset. It was only two thirty, but what else did I have to do that day?

I had mixed feelings about the Pinnacle. It was a gorgeous old hotel, built in the 1920s, all grand archways and intricate molding and sleek marble floors. I'd gone to the wedding of a Stanford classmate there, and had loved stopping off at the classic old bar. The beauty of the place, though, was undercut by two other experiences. My father had once done some electrical work for the hotel—he'd been hired as a subcontractor by a big Westside company—and the management had haggled

over the invoice. Then later, when my parents, in an in-
defatigable mixture of immigrant and blue-collar pride,
had wanted to have formal pictures taken there to mark
my twentieth birthday—coming-of-age day in Japan—
we had been escorted away from the front of the building by an overzealous security guard. My mother, in a
fit of admirable pique, had decided the photos would
be taken just over the property line—which they were,
with the hotel visible in the background, the security
guard keeping watch.

But today I walked into the lobby with no interfer-
ence and took the winding marble stairs up to the main
floor. I made my way to the bar and found a seat, glad to
blend in with all the anonymous people who happened
to be at the Pinnacle that day. Most of them were guests,
I figured, and maybe a few, like me, were stopping by
after events, enjoying a drink and a bit of elegance before heading back home or to work. The place was dark
and beautiful, straight out of some classic movie, with
elaborate chandeliers, gold fixtures, and velvet lamp-
shades. There was a shield flanked by matching cen-
taurs over the mantel of the bar, and figures of Neptune
and winged, bare-breasted nymphs were carved into the
stone columns. The bar itself was long and sleek, dark
wood encrusted with gold. There were big enveloping
chairs, and love seats, and several low tables; couples
and groups of four or five sat in these more private areas, heads bent over cocktails and nuts. I found a seat
at the bar and glanced up at the incongruous flat-screen
above the shelves of liquor; the Dodgers were playing a
preseason game.

I ordered a pint of Sam Adams and settled in, glad to

be away from the people at Fiona's luncheon, who gave such money and wielded such influence over matters about which most of them knew little. Once, twice, a burst of laughter from the other end of the bar—a group of young women, unfittingly loud for the venue—but I ignored them and turned to the screen.

I'd downed two-thirds of my beer when someone slid into the chair next to me. I knew who it was from the heightened energy in the air; I turned to find Fiona, looking as close to self-conscious as I'd ever seen her.

"Was it unbearable?" she asked.

"Hi," I said. Despite my earlier irritation, I was happy she was there. "No, it wasn't unbearable. Sorry—I had to get out of there."

"No, I'm sorry. I had to stay and talk to some people. I was hoping you'd still be here, and now here you are. I'm in need of a drink myself."

She ordered a martini, dry; when it arrived and she took her first sip of it, she visibly relaxed. Then she took another, bigger sip, and half the drink was gone.

"Tell me the truth, you hated it, didn't you? It was a bit much, I know. The speakers droned on for too long."

I smiled, amused that Fiona believed it was the speakers I was reacting to. "Mrs. Randall was surprisingly nice."

"Oh, Caroline," said Fiona, rolling her eyes. "She married into that money, you know."

I took a sip of my beer and didn't reply.

"You're not saying much. You didn't say much at the luncheon either. It makes me nervous when people don't talk."

"I was just observing," I said.

"You do that well."

There was a shout to the left of us, someone cheering a Dodgers hit; then an unrelated squeal from the girls at the end of the bar. Fiona flinched at both sounds, and it occurred to me how completely out of place she was here, out amongst regular people. This wasn't a dive or pickup joint, or even some trendy West Hollywood night spot; it was a classic, lovely bar, in a hotel that was once one of the most famous in LA. But even so, it was open to anyone, you didn't need a membership or a trust fund to get in the front door, and Fiona, in her custom-made $3,000 dress, looked as incongruous as a Bengal tiger in a dog pound. I liked seeing her off balance like this, and maybe I enjoyed it even more because of the lunch I'd just endured—though as soon as I was aware of this, I was quickly ashamed; I suddenly felt tender and protective.

"I don't know," she said now. She twisted the stem of her glass in her hand, and then turned in her seat to face me. "I keep thinking that by raising money for good causes, it's going to make a difference, it's going to *mean* something. My father tells me that we should only bet on winners—the established organizations, the museums and colleges. But it all feels so stodgy, so . . . *indirect*. Maybe he's right, though." She sighed. "I don't know what all this money and effort really amount to. He told me to quit dancing too, when I hit twenty-five—he said it was hurting my chance to get married and have kids. And I missed it, you know, I missed it terribly, and hated him. But it turns out that he was right."

I finished the last gulp of my beer and called the barkeep back over, ordering another martini for her and a bourbon, neat, for me. I swiveled in the stool to face her; we were almost knee to knee. "It was good, what you did today. It's good you're trying to make a difference."

But I knew that her reasons were different than the hostess's reasons; Caroline Randall's intentions were genuine and clear. And so what if she had married into her wealth? At least she knew what to do with it.

"You're sweet," Fiona said, then leaned forward, her knee brushing mine. "You know what? Janice, Kerry, and I are going to the Huntington on Thursday. You mentioned before that you like the Huntington—want to join us? No lectures, no fashion show, just enjoying an afternoon out."

I smiled. "Thanks, but I can't. Thursday's one of my scheduled days at Mrs. W—'s. I don't think she'd like it if I canceled."

"Do you always do what Mrs. W— says?"

"Do you always do what your father says?"

She leaned back and I couldn't read the look on her face. "Touché."

"I'm sorry," I said. "That was out of line." I refrained from saying the rest of it, which was that I didn't exactly have a perfect track record myself when it came to fathers. Just that week my mother had called to say my father was in bad spirits, his business was really taking a hit with the growth of the bigger companies. She didn't say—but I knew—that there were other worries behind that worry; her salary alone wasn't enough to cover their mortgage. She asked if I could visit, but I was too busy, I'd said, buried in dissertation work, although I hadn't touched those pages in weeks. In fact, I'd gathered them up and shoved them into the bottom of a file cabinet so they wouldn't be out and visible, taunting me.

Fiona shook her head and waved me off, eyes lowered. "No, you're absolutely right. I *have* done everything he's said. Went to Wellesley. Went to Julliard. Became a dancer. *Stopped* being a dancer. Married Aaron. Had a baby. And look where it's gotten me. Nowhere."

"You're not nowhere. You've got everything going for you."

And she did. Everyone loved her. She was attractive. She had an Ivy League degree and interesting work to do. And of course there was all that money. But suddenly I remembered something my mother had said after that awkward graduation weekend at Stanford: *You're too impressed with people whose greatest accomplishment was being born lucky.*

"Well, thank you, Richard, but it's hard to see what all of it adds up to. I want to *do* something. Useful. I want to have some impact on somebody."

"You do."

She smiled wryly. "You're nice," she said. And now she shifted in such a way that her knee brushed my leg again; I felt the heat of it shoot through my body. "You know, I was really glad you were there today. I'm glad you're here now."

"Me too."

There was another burst of laughter from the women at the end of the bar, enough to break the spell. Suddenly I remembered why I had come that day.

"So, I found out who the fourth person was," I said. "The other man in the accident."

Fiona drew back and looked at me intently. "Who?"

"A man named Jimmy Castillo. Do you know him?"

She looked perplexed. "Jimmy Castillo. No—never

heard of him. I don't know anyone named Castillo."

My heart sank—so this news wasn't as revelatory as I'd hoped.

"Are you sure?" Fiona asked. "How'd you find this out?"

"A friend of a friend who works up there, who knew about the accident."

"And this person's dependable?"

"I think so. He's one of the paramedics who responded to the call."

She was silent for a moment. "I just don't know a Castillo. He must have been a friend of the Larsons, maybe visiting from someplace else. But he's definitely not from LA."

I wondered how she could be so confident about this, so certain that, just because he wasn't part of her circle, he was from someplace else entirely. And her circle, I knew, was small—she and her peers not only lunched together, but traveled together, sent their children to the same exclusive schools.

"Maybe he was a friend of Steven J—'s," I ventured.

Fiona shook her head decisively. "No, I would have known." She turned the full force of her attention on me, light-blue eyes looking deep into my own, undoing me. "But this is wonderful, Richard. Thank you so much for finding out. I just wish . . ."

"What?" I leaned forward.

"I just wish we could figure out who this man *was*."

She looked at me searchingly, and I realized that this was the one thing I could do for her, the one area where her considerable resources and power didn't seem to be serving her much. It didn't occur to me to wonder why she wanted to know.

"Do you want me to keep looking around?" I asked.

"Yes. Could you?" She curved her hand over my knee and squeezed, then ran her fingers just a bit up my thigh. Our eyes met again. And it felt like the entire room tilted an inch, like everything had shifted. The man still nursed his beer behind me, the girls still laughed at the bar. But everything was different, and my breath caught in my throat and I couldn't think of a thing to say. Fiona smiled. She knew what she was doing to me.

I finally broke the eye contact and turned back to my drink. "Sure," I said, "I'll see what else I can find."

We finished our drinks, our conversation venturing back to the safer ground of the luncheon, only occasionally meeting each other's eyes. Eventually the check came, and she allowed me to pay; we walked out of the bar together.

"I'm downstairs," Fiona said. "I'll text my driver so he can pull around in front."

"Okay, I'll see you out."

"That's silly, go get in line for your car—it'll probably take half an hour."

I didn't tell her that I'd opted for the six-dollar parking across the street rather than the twenty-eight-dollar valet. "Well, at least to the elevator," I said. "If I have to wait anyway, I might as well walk you that far."

She shrugged, and sent her text, and then we walked together on the plush Oriental carpet, just a few people passing now, through the cavernous hall, under the ornately carved ceiling. I wasn't sure whether to offer my arm and decided against it, though I could feel her presence next to me, feel her warmth, and my heart beat a mile a minute. We turned into the elevator bank, which overlooked the bottom lobby; from below, the sounds of jazz floated up to us. We went over to the railing and looked down at that lovely space, and Fiona leaned against me, shoulder to shoulder, and covered my hand with her own. She smiled up at me now, and her look was unmistakable. Even through my disbelief, I knew that her signals were clear.

And so why didn't I lean over and kiss her? I had thought about it so many times, had ached with desire, and now here she was, presented to me, and I did nothing. Uncertain in other areas of my life, I usually wasn't hesitant with women. But looking at Fiona at that moment was like walking into a jewelry store whose goods I knew I couldn't afford. I wanted badly to handle the jewels, to feel their fineness in my fingers. But I was too afraid to touch. I had no right to them.

Then the metallic tone of the elevator arriving. I took a step back from her and said as calmly as I could, "Well, goodbye."

She stepped toward me again—she always stood too close—and quickly lifted her head up and kissed me. Her lips were warm and shocking; she kissed me gently, and then hard, her teeth sharp against my bottom lip. I heard the elevator door open as she reached up with her hand and touched my cheek and jaw. I lifted my own hands to hold her but she was already away from me and into the elevator. It was empty—how had she known it was going to be empty?—and she stepped to the very back of it and turned toward the front. The door began to slide shut again. "Goodbye," she said, smiling. And then she was gone.

CHAPTER SEVEN

I was moving quickly through Mrs. W—'s journals. By now she was in her early thirties; she'd married Baron J— and had given birth to two of her children. The descriptions of events hadn't gotten much more interesting, although her voice stayed consistently sassy. I had the odd sense that I was relating to two women: the Mrs. W— of today, and the one of her youth, whom I might know, at this point, better than she did. I'd gone through nine notebooks already, nearly seven hundred pages, and there were only three to go. Peeking ahead, I'd discerned that much of the final notebook was a history of her grandfather, an account of his life and career. But I didn't let myself skip forward. I wanted to read the journals in order, to reserve that story until I'd earned it. It occurred to me that the end of the project was in sight, which meant the end of everything that came with it—the afternoons at Casa del Cielo, the charity events, the reasons to see Fiona. I didn't want any of this to come to a close. I purposely slowed down my typing.

We had settled into a routine: I would read and transcribe for two hours or so, then break for lunch with Mrs. W— before working for another hour. Sometimes she would walk me through other wings of the mansion and talk about the paintings and sculptures she'd collected. Her tastes were eclectic, and ranged from classic to modern—van Gogh and Baldessari; Monet and Ruscha—and I slowly came to understand that she owned one of the finest collections in the city. She didn't seem to mind my near total ignorance of art; maybe I was indulging her in a way her children hadn't. And I drank up the attention, the education, which was all part of my improvement; which was preparing me to move more smoothly in her world.

One afternoon, as we sat on the patio and dined on shrimp salad, I presented her with a small wrapped package.

"A gift?" she asked, genuinely surprised. "For me?"

"Open it," I said, grinning. It was hard to find an appropriate gift for someone who had everything, but I thought she might enjoy this one. She tore open my barely competent wrapping and pulled out two costumes for her dogs—one designed like a bottle of white wine, the other a bottle of red.

"For Chardonnay and Pinot," I explained.

She laughed delightedly, and then I helped her gather the dogs, who stared up at me as I wiggled the costumes over their heads and then sat tolerantly on the patio to be admired. They looked ridiculous, and when Maria came out and saw them, she covered her mouth with her hand and giggled, which made Mrs. W— laugh all over again. I snapped a couple of pictures on my phone, so I could print one and have it framed.

Eventually we got back to eating lunch, and I described what I'd read that morning: her account of a fundraiser she'd attended for Richard Nixon in 1967, including her observation—several years before Watergate—that he seemed *sly and uncertain. Not a confident man. And unconfident men can be dangerous.*

"I'm a good reader of people," she explained, clearly pleased with herself, and with me for finding this.

"Apparently so!"

"But if you're up to 1967," she remarked, "you're two-thirds of the way through. I mean, not in my life, but in the notebooks."

"Your journal slows down in the late sixties," I acknowledged. "Why did you start writing less?"

She poked at her salad without looking up; for a moment I thought she hadn't heard me. "It was difficult, you know," she said finally, "when my children were young. I didn't have time for writing."

I left this alone, although I was aware of all the things she didn't mention—the death of her husband followed not long afterward by the loss of her parents; the quiet bearing of her burdens alone. It suddenly occurred to me that I'd never seen a picture of Baron J—. Maybe she kept one upstairs in her private quarters; maybe she stored all his likenesses away. Neither would have surprised me. By now I'd realized something about Mrs. W— and her ilk: the WASPs, like the Japanese, did not discuss their feelings.

"How long do you suppose it will take to finish?" she asked.

I thought about this. "Probably not more than three or four weeks."

"You'll have to stay on until the Founders' Luncheon," she said. The next month, on her birthday, she was going to be honored by the USC Founders Club, at the Ludlow Hotel in Beverly Hills. Clearly this was not just in recognition of her grandfather's gifts, but also for what they hoped she'd leave the school from her estate. She was looking forward to it, though, and her claims not to care about the honor were belied by how often she brought it up.

"I will," I promised. "I wouldn't miss it for the world."

"There's something else I'd like to discuss," she said, patting her mouth with a napkin. "Do you think . . . I wonder . . . What I mean to say is, I may have some other projects. Would you want to stay on here?"

I was caught off guard—not just by her question, but by what it implied. Whether it was out of affection, or the need for work to be done, or sheer loneliness, she wanted to keep me around.

"And I've been thinking," she continued. "You're such a bright young man. You could do anything, and yet you're stuck in that useless PhD program." She said *PhD* as if it were a mild disease. "Have you ever thought of doing something more practical? Like business or law?"

"I have," I said, although that wasn't really true. Or maybe it was true, as of that moment. "But it's a bit late to change course now. And I'm not really in a position to take out more loans."

"There's no need for loans. I could help, don't you see? And it's never too late—you're still very young. You could start at the law school or the business school in the fall!"

I sat up straight, startled, but also intrigued. I didn't bother to ask which school she meant. "That's very kind of you, Mrs. W—" I managed, truly touched. "But I couldn't. Besides, it's just not practical. Even if I wanted to go, applications were due last November."

She waved this away. "That doesn't matter. I could talk to the president."

"Mrs. W—, I know you have a lot of influence, but—"

"There are always special circumstances. And I'll simply remind him that I am the university's largest donor."

"I'm not sure that would help, Mrs. W—. I mean, I appreciate your offer, I really do. But money can't solve everything."

"Of course it can."

I sat thinking about this, sipping from my glass of iced tea. Mrs. W— softened now, and looked at me with an expression I hadn't seen before. "You've been such good company, Richard. I've enjoyed your being here."

"I've enjoyed it too," I said, afraid to meet her gaze. I looked around, my eyes falling on the second-story windows. I imagined Mrs. W— up there, in one of the many bedrooms, looking down at the patio, the garden, the spread of the city, entirely alone. Other than her staff, I realized, I was her only company.

"At any rate," she went on, sounding breezy again, "I just want you to live up to your potential. You could do so much more—don't you think?—than what you're doing."

During my next couple of sessions at Mrs. W—'s, I didn't get much work done. I kept thinking about the imminent end of my project and the prospect of losing all that came with it. Then I thought about her offers— of continued work, and of help shifting careers—and I would get overwhelmed, unable to contemplate either changing my life or going back to what it had been. Filing my dissertation away hadn't lessened its hold on me; I couldn't muster the will to get back to it, yet its presence seemed to grow, evidence of my lack of persistence. If I failed to complete it, I would be letting down my family—but turning away the chance for a better career might be worse.

One afternoon I sat, literally spinning in my leather chair, and found myself looking at the portraits on the wall, the paintings of the three young people. I'd assumed they were likenesses of Mrs. W— and her brother, and maybe a third relative, a cousin, because of how strange and old-fashioned they seemed. But now I realized they were paintings of her children. The eldest boy, Bart, looked stolid and decent, if a bit subdued. The girl was rather plain—not at all unpleasant, but without the beauty or self-possession of her mother. It must have been hard, I understood, to be Mrs. W—'s child, and especially her daughter. The younger boy—this had to be Steven—had an expression that seemed resentful and just short of angry. There was a flatness to his eyes that came across through all the years between now and when the paintings were done. It occurred to me that these were the only likenesses I'd seen of Mrs. W—'s children. They were locked in this room with only the company of her journals, as if already confined to her past.

I'd been sitting with the information Kevin had found about Steven's accident, not knowing what to do. I had no lead on Jimmy Castillo. Though as I began transcribing the tenth notebook under Steven's cold gaze, I wondered if I could find something related to *him* that might help shed light on the story. I already knew there was nothing in the house that hinted at his adult life. But maybe I could find out where he lived; maybe I could track down someone who knew him. I couldn't ask Maria or Lourdes, of course—that would be too suspicious. And when I googled his name, I found very little—just a record of the incident from the after-hours club many years ago, and a couple of mentions of him in connection to his mother. The only way to get more information was by snooping. And I needed more information. I told myself that I wasn't really prying too much, that finding out more about Steven was just filling in some blanks, fun sleuthing to complement my hired task. Yet I understood that Fiona probably wouldn't see me alone again until I had something more to tell her. And I could not stop thinking about her. I tossed and turned in bed, unable to sleep, tortured by unspent desire. I kept imagining our kiss at the Pinnacle; I should have followed her into the elevator and pressed her up against the wall.

And so I found myself, one Thursday afternoon, lingering in the hallway outside of Mrs. W—'s office. Mrs. W— was out at a gallery, shopping for art, and Lourdes was tidying up in the smallest of the three sitting rooms, the one that Mrs. W— actually used. I could hear her running the vacuum cleaner and that provided me cover as I gently turned the knob on the office door. I held my breath as if about to jump underwater, and dove in.

I'd been in this office once before, when Mrs. W— had gone in to retrieve some paperwork, but that time I had stayed in the doorway. I was there long enough, though, to realize that all her household and family matters were handled, tracked, processed, and documented here. In the top drawer of the desk, I knew, was the large accounting book where she kept track of household expenses; I'd seen her write out the regular check to me. She didn't lock the drawers or the door to the room— why should she? She had no reason to believe that anyone in her house had less than the best of intentions.

I also knew, because of Lourdes, that Mrs. W— kept family items here, and as I ventured farther into the room I was greeted with holiday cards and photographs of five different young adults, presumably grandchildren, all with variations of the high, broad cheeks and narrow jaws that marked them as members of the W— clan. There were two photographs of a grown man in a ranch setting, wearing a cowboy hat and plaid shirt. I recognized him as her first son, Bart. There were pictures, as well, of a middle-aged woman who shared certain features with Mrs. W—: the cheekbones and jaw, a certain tilt of the head. Yet this woman seemed a diminished version of her, as if made from leftover material. So, Bart and Jessica were here, and all of their children. But there were no pictures of a third adult child. No pictures of Steven.

I listened to make sure that the vacuum was still going and then ducked down, suddenly aware that someone working in the garden might see me through the window. I sat hurriedly in Mrs. W—'s hard-backed chair to get out of the line of sight. What was it like to sit in that chair, and to contemplate and distribute such wealth? I couldn't begin to imagine. Carefully I opened the bottom file drawer, wondering if this was where she kept records of her children.

The drawer held a dozen or so hanging files that were filled with individual folders, all neatly labeled with names of financial institutions and funds. I pulled out one of these and looked at a quarterly statement; just this one account contained more than enough to pay for USC's most recent building renovation. I replaced that folder and rifled through the others. Nothing personal or family-related here.

There was an accordion folder lodged in the back of the drawer; I gave it a tug and pulled it out. Inside were envelopes, maybe three or four dozen. I assumed they were for Mrs. W—, sent from banks or business associates, but when I tipped the folder open and the envelopes scattered on the desk, they were older than I'd thought. Much older—dated 1911, 1905, 1921. Addressed not to Mrs. W—, but to Langley. The envelopes were in good shape despite being a century old; when I opened them, I saw the letters were too.

Mr. W—, one said, written in a shaky, unlearned hand, *thank you for paying off the note on our farm house. You say the wool from our sheep helped your mother make clothes last winter, but we was just being good neighbors to one whos always been good to us. You are a true gentleman.*

Dear Langley, said another, *I simply cannot get over your generosity, and neither, truth be told, can the rest of this town. It's one thing to purchase enough wood for the people to make it through winter. It's another to tell me that I was charging too low a price and to pay nearly twice what I asked. Your generosity not only helped the townsfolk get through the season, it saved my logging operation and mill, and thus dozens of jobs.*

Sir, one of them said simply, *when I came back from the war and lost my leg, I did not know how I would manage. Thank you for giving me a job with your company. It has made it possible for me to stay home in Bakersfield, and to care for my wife and young son.*

To Langley W—, said one from 1921, I grew up in the Magnolia Home for Boys. I met you when you came out to the home to donate land for our new football field. Some other boys were teasing me because I didn't want to play. You told me not to despair, that every man had a purpose, and that those of us who'd lost our parents must be particularly strong for God to have placed upon us such a burden. You have no idea how much your kindness meant to me. I went to college and then law school at the University of Southern California, and now I am an attorney in Los Angeles. Had it not been for the Magnolia Home and your encouragement, sir, I shudder to think what would have become of me.

Mr. W—, said the last one I read, written in pencil, I know it is of no use to write you now that you're gone. But when I went to pay my respects at your funeral, they turned me and other workingmen away. So let me thank you in the only way I can and hope the message reaches you or your family somehow. You gave me a chance years ago on a drill site in Kern County, when others thought I was too scrawny to work. That was the first step that led to my own business, manufacturing drilling cable. You wouldn't remember me anyway, but I will always remember you. I remember you sitting down next to me one day when I was eating lunch, when I was tired and discouraged and didn't think I could keep on. And you told me it was always hard at first, but that I should buck up, because you knew I could do it, you saw something in me, and that helped me see something in myself.

These letters struck me differently than the self-serving accounts in Langley's book, the one compiled by the Colonial Club. They described a man consistent with the grandfather in the postcard—which I'd safely returned to Mrs. W—'s journal. I was now about ready to transcribe the final notebook, which documented more of his story, and I was eager to learn about the contours of the world in which this larger-than-life figure had moved. It occurred to me that part of Langley's decency, which I believed was real, was due to his having been poor and, more importantly, to his remembering what being poor had been like. He lived well, yes, but he never forgot. His descendants, on the other hand, had never known.

I spun around and looked at the small bookshelf, searching for more documents, but it didn't yield what I sought. It held more photographs, and books on artists and history, a picture book of garden estates. I listened to make sure the vacuum was still going—it was. I turned back to the desk and opened the top drawer now, the one that held the checks, and pulled out a photo album–sized ledger. There were records of checks written out to me, and to Lourdes and the other household staff; doing some quick calculations, I saw that Lourdes made more than most teachers or cops. There were some other checks that appeared to be made out to insurance companies on behalf of the staff; then a large check—$36,000—marked, *Blakely School, Virginia*. I wondered at this; none of Mrs. W—'s grandchildren went to school in Los Angeles, so why would she be paying tuition to the swankiest girls' school in the city? Then I realized: Lourdes's eight-year-old daughter was named Virginia. Mrs. W— was full of surprises.

Beneath the first ledger there were two others, leather-bound and smaller. I lifted them out and opened the cover of the one on top. It was a record of Mrs. W—'s charitable donations—some that I recognized, including one to the children's hospital in Santa Monica, but many more I didn't. Scanning through the record, I saw a number of six-figure donations, as well as a couple at seven figures, to children's charities, arts organizations, research centers, schools, as well as animal and wildlife organizations, a few conservation efforts, and—most surprisingly—a legal aid organization for immigrants. This last, I realized, was the place that helped Maria. All of these donations had been unknown to me—and, I understood, to everyone else as well.

I put this ledger aside and opened the last one, where I found handwritten records of particularly large payments, earnings, and transfers—2.3 million dollars in dividends here, a payment of 10.4 million for a property there. This seemed to be the record of even bigger-ticket items, not charity-related, which was borne out by the other items I saw: a deposit of eight million from another account; a payment of four million for a house in Montecito. There were not many entries, and the dates were far apart—there'd been fewer than thirty entries since 2005.

Then I saw something that caught my eye—a payment of twenty million dollars to something called *First Quarter*, dated May 24, 2009. That was a month after the accident at Cliffhaven. And just a few weeks later, on July 2, a transfer to the account of Steven J— in the amount of two hundred and fifty million dollars.

Why such huge amounts of money? I wondered. I knew Steven had been severely injured, maybe paralyzed—but still, this seemed like more than it would have cost to nurse him back to health, to sustain him as he recovered. Was First Quarter some kind of rehabilitation facility? And how, given his mother's almost unthinkable generosity, could Steven fail to be in touch with her now? I didn't know, and yet I knew I had *something*—that there was meaning here I couldn't yet see. And so I took out my phone and snapped pictures of both of the entries. Then I put the ledgers back in the drawer and slipped out of the room.

That night, I spent two hours searching the Internet and found next to nothing. There were several sporting goods shops called First Quarter throughout the country, even a coin-collecting operation. But the First Quarter I was looking for wasn't either of these. All I could determine was that there was some kind of business called First Quarter in Paso Robles. That had to be the place. There was nothing but a PO box listed as an address, no indication of what it did or whom it belonged to.

Still, I knew I was on to something, and the more I contemplated that check as well as the huge transfer of money to Steven, the more I was convinced it was not a coincidence. I was starting to think I needed to take a trip to the Central Coast. But first I wanted to tell Fiona.

I was vaguely aware that sharing what I'd found was venturing further into questionable territory, yet I was too caught up in Fiona to care. It didn't register then that I was also acting against my own best interests. I should have remembered what Janet, the card shark, had said about why she avoided solitaire: when you play yourself, she told me once, you almost always lose.

The next afternoon I texted Fiona around two o'clock, figuring she'd be done or nearly done with whatever luncheon she had that day. *I have something*, I wrote cryptically. And this time, instead of the buzz of a text, the music of an incoming call.

"What is it?" she asked without identifying herself.

"Hello, Fiona," I said. "How are you doing?"

"Oh, come *on*," she said, laughing, "don't be a tease. What did you find?"

"A couple of money transfers around the time of the accident. Big ones. One of them to Steven."

"Are there records? Did you get copies?"

"No—I took pictures of them, though."

"On your phone?"

"Yes."

"Send them to me."

I hesitated. Letting them out of my possession didn't feel right; giving them to Fiona would be a bigger violation than the one I'd already committed. "I'd rather show them to you."

She didn't miss a beat: "Okay, why don't you come meet me?"

My heart started pounding. "Now?"

"Yes, now!" She laughed again.

"Where are you?"

"At the Beach Club," she said, naming another private club that I'd never known existed until a few months before and now had been to several times. "But don't come here. Meet me at the Bismarck, in the bar."

I put on a dress shirt and a pair of gray pants and headed over to Santa Monica. The traffic on the 10 was already sluggish, and it took me an hour to get there. The hotel was on a bluff overlooking the beach; it was huge, stately, and ornate. It stood like a castle, surrounded by greenery and iron fences, and after I turned into the gated driveway, I relinquished my old car to the suited valet. As soon as I could, I promised myself, I'd get a better car.

I followed the signs for the bar, scanning the indoor seats and the spacious outdoor patio. No sign of Fiona. I asked a waitress if there was another bar, which there was, and I checked there too—a darker, more private place—though she wasn't there either. Finally I texted: *I'm in the bar now, where are you?*

And my phone lit up with the answer: *In the bar in the presidential suite. Twenty-fourth floor.*

Of course she'd be in a more removed location, separate from the public. I took the elevator up to the twenty-fourth floor, imagining a tiny, private space of three or four tables, as I'd now seen in several other posh hotels. Yet when I disembarked from the elevator and approached the door of the suite, it looked like a regular hotel room, and there was no doorman stationed in front. I knocked, and Fiona answered, smiling. She was wearing a blue-green sundress that clung to her body and set off the blue of her eyes. Her hair was down, flowing over her shoulders; her arms and legs were totally bare.

"Come in," she said. "It's a beautiful day." She took my arm and ushered me into a huge set of rooms that probably occupied half the floor. There were windows on three sides, and a patio that looked out at a gorgeous view of the ocean.

"Where's . . . ?" I started.

She led me over to a high counter with a couple of stools and ceremoniously sat me down. "The bar," she said. "At the presidential suite."

I still wasn't sure what to make of this—there were several other rooms, and through an open doorway I saw a cool, spacious bed, covered with a light white comforter. Maybe some of her girlfriends were here, or somebody else. As if she read my mind, she said, "I'm alone. I took the suite for the night. Sometimes I sneak away and spend a night in a hotel, when everything gets to be too much."

"And your family?" I asked.

"They're understanding. I can be a royal bitch when I get stressed or overtired, so my husband is *very* supportive of me going off by myself to recharge."

She smiled at me, and there was something in the way she lifted one side of her mouth, the way she held my eyes, that suddenly made me aware that we were alone in a hotel suite together, hidden away and unaccounted for. My heart began to thump so hard I was sure she could see it through my shirt. I was afraid to move, and afraid not to, and she gave a small, flirtatious laugh, as if she knew exactly what kinds of knots she was tying me up in.

"Want a drink?" she offered, and before I replied she'd poured me a bourbon and herself a glass of wine. We toasted each other across the bar. I took two mid-sized gulps, the burning sensation dulling my nerves a bit, before she asked, "Why don't you show me what you've got?" I must have looked startled, because she threw her head back and laughed. "The pictures, silly. The records of the payments."

I took my phone out of my pocket, opened up the photo of one of the records, and handed it to her. She leaned over the bar, revealing enough for me to see she wasn't wearing a bra, and held the phone like a piece of precious evidence.

"What the hell is First Quarter?" she asked.

"I don't know. I was hoping you could tell me."

"Never heard of it. But twenty million dollars. And then . . . my God!" She'd just scrolled over to the picture of the payment to Steven. She looked up at me, then back at the phone again. "Two hundred and fifty million dollars?"

"I know. Can you believe it? The only thing I can think of is that it's all related to his care. He was badly injured, right?"

"Yes. But that doesn't explain it. And it's not like he really needs this money—he's already got a trust fund."

"Well, I don't know, but I think there's something there." And then, loosened by the alcohol and the proximity of Fiona, I said, "Maybe I should take a trip up to the Central Coast."

She put the phone down on the bar and took my hand. "Really?"

"I'm thinking about it," I said. The warmth of her touch moved up my arm and radiated through my body. "Between those payments and figuring out who Jimmy Castillo is, it might make sense to go there in person." Did it really? Maybe. But what else did I have to do? I was a graduate student with no real commitments, beyond my few hours a week with Mrs. W—; no one would care or even notice if I was gone. It would probably do me good to get away for a couple of days. I was so caught up in Fiona that I couldn't get my own work done, anyway. "I'd have to rearrange my schedule, but I don't think I can get much further without going up there and digging around. Cambria's probably the best bet, since it's the closest town to Cliffhaven."

She stroked my hand, not acknowledging what I knew we both knew: that she could never go to a public place and be inconspicuous. "You did well, Richard." And now she smiled, showing perfect white teeth. "This is fun."

It *was* fun. I loved pleasing her. I loved making her smile. And I loved unearthing information that was related to present-day events, rather than obscure but useless facts to be examined, analyzed, and stuffed into a boring dissertation that no one except my advisors would ever read.

It became more fun when Fiona poured us another round of drinks and we ventured out to the patio. It was a beautiful afternoon—midseventies, the sky still April-clear. The entire coast of Southern California was spread out before us—the land curving out along the Palos Verdes Peninsula and again to the north toward Malibu; Catalina Island green and welcoming in the distance. On that patio we were well above the next-highest buildings; we were alone with the wind and the birds. I loved how the breeze played with Fiona's blond hair; the way the sun shone on her skin. We pointed out seagulls, a boat sailing on the horizon, an airplane trailing an advertisement. With each new sighting Fiona grabbed my hand or pressed her bare shoulder against my arm, and finally, when the sea and the sun and the bourbon were all mixed up together, I turned her toward me by the shoulders and kissed her. She drew back, giggling, and then kissed me in return, all laughter gone now as our bodies bent toward each other and the air around us changed.

So what was it like to make love to the woman I'd

dreamed about for months? I wish I could say it was earth-shattering, transcendent—that it lived up to my most precious imaginings. But as we moved from the patio to the bed with its white-white covers, I felt a resistance in Fiona, a holding ground, even as her body gave way; even as she—with seeming fervor—undid my shirt and my pants and pulled me down on top of her. The heat of our bodies couldn't dislodge the undercurrent of cold; it was like making love to an ice floe, frozen and unreachable. When it was over—which happened quickly—it was almost a relief, and we didn't look at each other for several moments. I had no business being there, I thought again; she was way beyond my reach. But then we started again, slowly and much more in sync, and I took the time to linger.

At one point, Fiona stopped me and held my face in both her hands. "You are beautiful," she said huskily.

"So are you."

Two, three hours afterward we lay tangled in the sheets, the ocean breeze coming in through the open windows. The sun had started its inexorable lowering, casting a golden light on the dark-green hills, and for a while I watched Fiona's face as she slept, unbelieving of my luck. It was amazing that this woman was lying here beside me. Had I found myself sharing a bed with a princess or a movie goddess, I would not have felt more wonder or reverence.

As I looked at her, out of nowhere I remembered a conversation I'd had with Kevin and Rosanna. After Kevin had seen the condition of my apartment a couple of weeks before, they'd invited me over for a home-cooked meal. As Rosanna worked over a pan of chicken and onions, Kevin cajoled me into showing him a picture of, as he put it, my "new lady." He didn't have to push very hard. I'd wanted to show her off, and with a slight feeling of self-consciousness, of claiming too much, I called up a picture from one of the photograph services that always came to society functions. In it, Fiona wore a shimmery black dress, and she posed with one hand on her hip.

Kevin whistled. "Very nice," he said, mock-punching me on the shoulder. "Very classy."

"Let me see!" Rosanna called out from the kitchen, demanding the phone. Kevin snatched it from my hand and took it over to her, ignoring my protests. She stared at the image, spatula still suspended over her pan, then leaned in for a closer look. "She's had a lot of work done, huh?"

"What do you mean?" I said.

"To her face. Botox, her lips, maybe some tucking around the eyes."

"Really?" I was genuinely surprised, thinking Rosanna was just jealous. "How can you tell?"

She snorted. "How can you *not*?"

But watching Fiona now, as she lay still, I saw no signs of what Rosanna was talking about. She must have made it up, I decided. Fiona looked perfect to me.

We ordered room service and lounged around in our robes, feeding each other filet mignon and strawberries. We drank a bottle and a half of champagne and watched the sunset, took a long, sloppy bubble bath, and then made love again until we passed out.

When I finally awoke the next morning, Fiona wasn't in bed; I stumbled out to the main room to find her fully dressed, completely put back together, as if the last afternoon and night had never happened.

She smiled and came over to give me a kiss. "Look at you, you sleepy bear. You're very cute. But I have to go. A meeting in Century City at ten o'clock."

She couldn't stay for breakfast, not even a cup of coffee. I tried to suppress my disappointment.

"Thank you for the wonderful, wonderful night," she said, kissing me, flicking her tongue between my lips. Then she walked out the door, not bothering to look back.

CHAPTER EIGHT

The Central Coast has long been my favorite escape, ever since I went there the summer after high school. My friends and I had stayed in a busy campground in Big Sur, and after that I'd returned almost every year—sometimes back to Big Sur, but more often, especially with girlfriends, to one of the modest, low-key inns in the artsy little tourist town of Cambria. It was close enough that I could take off on a Friday afternoon and arrive in time for dinner, far enough that it felt like we were really getting out of Los Angeles. The coast was wilder north of Santa Barbara, moody and untamed, devoid of the sun bunnies who choked the wide, bland beaches of Southern California. I'd gone up to Big Sur or Cambria at several key moments in my life—when I had to decide whether to leave California for grad school; when I finally told my father that I wasn't interested in the family business. And last year I'd come up to spend a weekend with Chloe, supposedly to celebrate my birthday, but really as part of a last-ditch effort to save our faltering relationship.

It had been overcast most of the weekend, foggy and haunted-feeling; when Chloe and I walked along the boardwalk on Moonstone Beach, we couldn't even see the water. We ventured down the rotting wooden stairs and onto the sand, and as the fog began to lift,

we scanned the beach for the colorful stones it was famous for, and the wet black cliffs for mussels, all under the eye of an imperious sea lion, who sprawled on
a rock just off shore. Later we drove up the coast to see
the elephant seals, the huge, obese, Jabba the Hutt–like
creatures that congregated at this particular beach by
the hundreds every spring—massive piles of dark flesh
protecting their young, most of them lying motionless
on the cliff-enclosed beach, completely still except for
the flicking of their dexterous fins, which sent sprays
of cooling sand over their bodies. The males engaged
in loud and spectacular battles, lifting their elongated
snouts and slamming their necks together. It was impressive and somewhat comical to watch them in action,
and I loved to bring people who'd never seen them.

But when I took Chloe that weekend, the always-
rancid smell of the giant beasts was particularly bad, and
when we looked directly below us from the edge of the
cliff, we saw a huge, bloated, light-colored corpse, well
into the process of decay, with three seagulls perched on
its barrel chest and feasting on the flesh of its belly. Its
intestines and organs were mixed in a gruesome colorful
stew; one determined bird pulled on a string of purple
innard until it snapped free. Chloe covered her mouth
and let out a cry, and I led her down the walkway to our
car. On the way back to our hotel room, and long afterward, the stench still filled our nostrils. We went to bed
that night without eating dinner. When we got back to
LA, she moved out.

I hadn't been to the Central Coast since Chloe and I had
split, and so it was with a sense of dread and heaviness

that I started my trip, leaving LA around ten o'clock on a Tuesday morning to avoid commuter traffic. I'd told Mrs. W— on Monday that I had some unavoidable commitments at school, and she'd been fine with me missing a day; I'd go to her house, as scheduled, on Friday. As I drove north and west on the 101, the browning hills and wide valleys of Southern California gave way to greener and wilder land; the cities receded to reveal small, far-flung enclaves of houses; and the highway stretched directly beside the ocean. Somewhere north of Santa Barbara I looked left and saw half a dozen shiny crescents, which I realized were dolphins. Despite my thoughts of Chloe, I felt the relief and lightening that I always felt when the concrete dropped away and the landscape changed. This sense of calm only deepened as I continued north through sprawling farmland, where the last of the California poppies and lupines of spring still dotted the hillsides orange and purple; as the dramatic bluffs and rocks of the Central Coast came into view; as I saw the first groupings of dark, lush Monterey pines, which didn't grow in the warmer climate to the south. I made it to Cambria in just over four hours and checked in at a hotel along Moonstone Beach, purposely avoiding the nicer place where Chloe and I had lodged in favor of the cheaper one I'd often stayed in on my own.

After I dropped off my overnight bag, I walked across the street to the boardwalk and stood looking out at the gorgeous beach and churning blue ocean, the sun glinting brightly off the water. I closed my eyes and breathed in the fresh sea air. For a moment I fantasized about Fiona being there with me, her hair loosened—as I had now finally seen it—and blowing in the wind. I remembered cupping my hands over her shoulders; I remembered the taste of her skin. But she would never, I realized, stay in a place like the one I was staying in, just like she'd never visit me in Jefferson Park, and so I pushed the thought out of my mind. It was close to three o'clock. If I went into town I'd have time to ask around at several places before dinner.

I got in my car and drove back across Highway 1 to the west part of the village, one of two separate mile-long strips of restaurants, galleries, and tourist shops, many in cottage-style buildings, that were choked with tourists on the weekends. But it was quiet on this Tuesday. I went first to the local market that carried organic, high-end fare, fresh seafood and meat; if Jimmy Castillo was part of some established wealthy family, they might shop here—if they did their own shopping at all. I asked the aging, bearded hippie at the first register if he'd heard of him. I was, I said, a friend from high school just passing through town. The guy shook his head and suggested a couple of other places—the fancy pet store, an art gallery, the one auto repair place in town, where everyone—homeowner or worker, wealthy or poor—had no choice but to take their cars. I went to those places and was met with a succession of no's, accompanied by confused, uncomprehending looks or glares of suspicion.

Finally I got a coffee and sat down on a bench in front of a store that carried goods that no one needed, kitschy beach-related decorations and home furnishings. The people who lived in Cambria or who had the kind of money the Larsons did would never shop here, I realized. It was too expensive for the workers who made the restaurants and businesses run, too cheesy and clogged with tourists for the wealthy.

Still, I had no other way of tracking down the man I sought, and so I tried some different places—the gas station, an ice cream parlor. No luck. Eventually, close to six o'clock, I was lured into the barbecue joint I always visited when I was in town; its kitchen opened wickedly onto the street and expelled the irresistible smell of cooking meat. There was a large outdoor patio area, but the inside was cavernous too, with the added benefit of large-screen TVs that were always set to sports stations. I decided to buy a rack of barbecued pork ribs and watch whatever game was on TV. It struck me, as it always did, that the place didn't know whether it wanted to be a sports bar or a surfer hangout. The walls were decorated both with surfboards and framed jerseys of pro baseball and football players. The huge menu display behind the counter offered only a few items: a variety of meat and a couple of sides. I placed my order with a shaggy-haired kid whose quick, precise movements and self-possessed air suggested he was a local.

When he handed me my change, I asked, "Hey, do you happen to know a guy named Jimmy Castillo?" A cloud came over his face—pay dirt—and I quickly explained, "We have a mutual friend who went to high school with him, and she wanted me to ask after him."

"She went to Paso High?" the kid asked. His name tag said *Craig*. "What was her name?"

"Pamela Erickson," I responded, glad that I hadn't told this kid what I'd told the others—that it was I who'd gone to high school with Jimmy. My lack of knowledge of the area would have been quickly obvious. "I think you're too young to have known her."

"She doesn't know then, does she?" the kid said, sounding troubled. "She doesn't know about what happened to Jimmy."

"No," I said, trying not to sound too interested. "What happened?"

"He was in a bad accident." Another customer came up behind me, but when he saw the look on Craig's face, he moved on to another register. "Up at Cliffhaven. A couple of people died, but Jimmy survived, and he's pretty messed up now. No one really knows much about it. I only know because my dad works on a ranch near where Jimmy used to work. He says Jimmy was the best horse trainer he'd ever seen."

"He's a horse trainer?" I asked, forgetting I was supposed to know who he was.

"Yeah," the kid said, now looking at me funny. "Didn't Pamela tell you? That's why he was living on the Larson estate. He trained their horses."

I glanced away from the kid—back at the men laboring in the open kitchen, all Latino, in white cook's clothing—trying to cover my surprise. So Jimmy Castillo had *worked* for the Larsons. Of course—I should have known.

"Does he still live in the area?" I asked.

Craig nodded. "He lives with his parents over near Paso—they take care of him. No one's seen him since the accident. But you might be able to find out more from his sister Lorena. She works down at the Anchor Café, on Moonstone Beach."

"Lorena," I repeated. "At the Anchor Café." Now my heart was racing. I had an actual lead, a person to talk to. "Thanks, man. I appreciate it." I turned and walked away, intent on going to the Anchor immediately.

"Hey!" Craig shouted as I was halfway to the door. "Hey, don't you want your food?"

I drove back across Highway 1 and over to Moonstone Beach, along the same string of restaurants, inns, and hotels where I was staying. The Anchor Café was one of the first places on the main part of the drive, about four doors down from my motel. Leaving my bag of takeout on the passenger seat—I was too worked up to eat—I parked and went inside. It was one of those casual beachfront restaurants you might find anywhere along the coast, dark, weathered wood on the outside and decorated with ocean themes within—fishing nets draped from the ceiling, three-and four-foot taxidermy fish attached to the walls and swimming between wooden ships wheels, sand stars, and crabs. There was an eight-foot-tall replica of a lighthouse dominating one corner, facing a stone fireplace that at the moment held no fire. But the tables were full, occupied by families and groups who were speaking loudly, adding to a general sense of liveliness. A young blond woman in a short-sleeve blue uniformed top appeared at the front desk, asked if I was dining alone.

"Actually, I'm looking for someone," I said. "Is Lorena working tonight?"

"No, it's her night off," the girl answered. Her name tag read *Paula*. "But I promise Justine will take good care of you!"

"Oh, no, thanks. I was just coming in to say hi to Lorena. When is she working again?"

"I think tomorrow. Let me check." And she pulled up something on a computer screen in front of her, clicked the mouse a few times. "Yup, breakfast through lunch. She'll be here from seven to three."

I thanked her and drove back to my motel. When I finally got into my room, I realized how tired I was—the drive, the asking around about Jimmy Castillo, the excitement and anticipation of learning about his sister, the disappointment of not immediately finding her. But it was probably for the best. In the morning, I'd be less exhausted and more clear-headed. I went to bed and slept a dreamless sleep.

The next morning I woke up at nine—I'd slept eleven hours—with the unfamiliar urge to go for a run. I'd used to run and bike regularly, but my body had gone to shit in that long post-breakup era of total inertia; of too much beer and unhealthy food. It had been so long since I'd exercised that I'd almost forgotten the high that physical activity could bring, the relief and sense of well-being. But there was something about waking up to the sound of the ocean, the cool fresh air, that made me want to get up and get moving.

And so I did—improvising with my sneakers and the sweats I'd brought to sleep in, jogging slowly up Moonstone Drive. At the inlet I left the road and scrambled down to the beach and kept running on the wet packed sand. There was no one out there except for the seagulls, and the fresh air washed me clean. To my left the ocean crashed dramatically. In front of me lay the Big Sur coast, the green mountains jutting up against the sea. I struggled on, winded, yet feeling alive. A half-mile up the beach I saw three gray pelicans, huge prehistoric things, flying low over the water. They flew single file, in perfect synchronized movement, dipping and rising with the waves. It was gorgeous here. The hills extended into the ocean like the tide in reverse, waves of land pushing out into the water. What secrets this land must have held. A few miles to the north stood Cliffhaven, where Steven J— and Jimmy Castillo had nearly been killed, where Charles Larson and his son had lost their lives. I squinted and tried to discern a structure on one of the hills, but the tops of them were obscured by the morning fog, and I saw nothing but the land itself, immovable and silent, folding endlessly into the distance.

At twelve thirty I walked down to the Anchor Café. A middle-aged man was at the front desk now, and he led me to a table at the window. The place looked different than it had the night before, all the decorations a little more dusty and worn, a bit tacky, in the daylight. Only four of the tables were occupied, and the diners were quieter than the previous night's bunch. One waitress seemed to have responsibility for the whole floor now, and when she passed by I looked at her name tag: *Lorena*.

I'd planned to ask about her brother right away, but suddenly it was obvious that doing so would be startling, unkind. Plus I wanted to get a sense of who Lorena was. She looked young, midtwenties. She was of average height, with skin the color of wet sand, and black hair pulled back into a ponytail that flicked one way and then another whenever she switched directions. She was sturdily built—not heavy or even stocky by any means, but not skinny either—no-nonsense, ready for sport or work, no artificial gym-sculpted body. As she delivered plates and picked up empty ones, she was efficient and polite, but not overly so. When she finally came over to my table I got my first look at her eyes—lovely liquid-brown eyes—which seemed a decade or two older than the rest of her.

"Are you ready to order?" she asked, not brusquely, but not messing around either. "Or do you still need a minute?" She had a surprisingly even and resonant voice, no girlish trill, and I sat feeling the significance of having tracked her down and almost forgot to reply.

"Uh, yes," I managed finally. "A burger please."

"Would you like something to start? A salad or some chowder? The chowder is our specialty."

"Sure, a cup of chowder, please," I said, and then she was gone.

She brought the chowder shortly with the same businesslike efficiency, and the burger ten minutes later, allowing a tiny smile as she set the plate down. A middle-aged couple was seated at the table behind me and they engaged her in conversation—yes, she was from the area, she told them; she'd grown up near Paso Robles; her family still lived there and worked on a ranch. She'd gone off to college—Cal Poly, San Luis Obispo—and had come back after graduation; she lived down in Morro Bay with some friends from school.

I ate my burger quickly—I was hungry from my run—and ordered coffee to prolong my stay. Soon Lorena brought me my check. I could say something now or I could let her walk away without her knowing I'd come there to see her. For just a second I wondered if it might be better that way—sometimes, even now, I still wonder. But I'd driven all the way up there to find out about her brother, and so I touched her on the arm as she was turning away, and said, "Excuse me, I'm sorry. But are you Jimmy Castillo's sister?"

She pulled back as if she'd been burned. "I might be," she answered suspiciously. "Who wants to know?"

"My name's Rick Nagano," I said stupidly, as if this would explain anything. "I'm sorry, I don't mean to startle you. But I wanted to talk with you about his accident."

Her mouth twisted into a grimace and I saw the pain in her eyes; all the carefully built artifice, the stalwart defense, had crumbled at the mention of her brother. "Why do you want to talk about that?" She almost spat it at me. "Nothing can be done to change it. Besides, *no one* wants to talk about the accident."

I didn't know what this meant, but sensed an opening. "There's someone who's very interested in finding out what happened."

"You mean what *really* happened?"

So there *was* something more, something worth finding out. I leaned forward now and looked her in the eye; I spoke in a low and confidential tone. "Yes, what really happened. Can we talk?"

She glared at me. A red flush had come up on both of her cheeks and covered her neck and chest. "Why the hell should I talk to *you*?"

"Because I want to know. Maybe . . . maybe I can help." This was blatantly false—there was nothing I could do that would be of use. But that was all I could think of to say.

She snorted. "Help. Jimmy's had just about all the help he can take."

I didn't say anything, but I noticed people from a couple of other tables looking over at us—either because they heard the tone of her voice, or because they needed service.

Lorena sensed this too. She came back to herself and looked at me. "I get off at three," she said, standing up straight again. "Meet me at the Sand Bar."

The Sand Bar was another restaurant about a half-mile farther up Moonstone Drive—a place, I knew from previous trips, of mediocre food and indifferent service. What it boasted, though, was a large patio overlooking the ocean. There were twenty or twenty-five tables set up outside, though the real attraction was the bar-like counter that stretched the entire length of the patio, facing west. I'd spent several evenings there, over the years, watching the sun set over the horizon. But on this day, I chose a table set back from the counter so Lorena and I could look at each other. I settled in one of the chairs that faced the water, in a bit of shade provided by an umbrella.

I realized almost immediately why she'd suggested we meet there. The place was busy, even at what should have been the outer edge of lunch. The crowd and the noise would provide more privacy than some quieter place, where our conversation might be overheard. Three o'clock came and went, and then three fifteen, and I started to wonder if maybe she'd decided not to come. But then, just after three thirty, I saw her walking toward my table. She'd changed out of her short-sleeve work shirt and was now wearing a black button-down top. As she sat, I again felt the incongruity of how young she looked physically and how old she seemed.

"I almost didn't come," she said by way of greeting.

"I'm glad you did."

A waiter appeared, a guy about my age who, surprisingly, for such a small town, didn't seem to know Lorena. I'd been nursing a beer and now she ordered one too; we both declined the offer of food.

We sat in awkward silence, our own quiet somehow magnified by the din all around us. There was a particularly loud burst of laughter from the group of six seated just to our left. I stole a peek at her. Sitting down, she seemed smaller than she had when she was working.

"I overheard you talking with another table at the Anchor earlier," I eventually said. "So, your family's from Paso Robles?"

But if I'd thought that her family origins were a safer topic to begin with, or a good distraction, I was wrong.

"Yes, and I'm never moving back. Why do you want to know about my brother?"

I felt a bit assailed, put back on my heels, but I leaned forward, as if into the wind. For all of Lorena's understandable suspicion, she had some kind of knowledge, some information I needed, and the thought of unearthing it, of bringing it back to Fiona, gave me the strength to withstand her resistance.

"Well, first of all," I asked, "how is he doing?"

Lorena looked at me, confused, a bit incredulous. "How is he doing? He's paralyzed from the neck down, and he's in his bed most of the day, except when my mother and his nurse decide to lift him into a wheelchair. He needs to be fed and bathed and wiped. And his brain was scrambled too, so he doesn't know what's going on half the time. So I'd have to say he's doing pretty shitty."

Just then the waiter reappeared with Lorena's beer, and we sat in silence until he was gone. She took a big gulp of it—downing a third all at once—then glanced at me, and looked away.

I deserved this anger, I knew. My question had come from obligatory politeness, not real concern. I had to do better. "That's awful," I said, more gently now. "He's living with your parents?"

Lorena nodded. "Yes. He's married, you know. With a son and a daughter. But Ana's still so messed up about it that she can't see him without crying, and it's hard to have the kids around him. My parents have a whole setup in their new house—a room for him, a special bed, a full-time caregiver. Ana and the kids visit him every weekend. Sometimes he can have a normal conversation, and sometimes he doesn't even know who they are. It's pretty fucking sad, to tell you the truth."

I didn't know what to say to this. What could I say? Above us, a seagull flew perilously close, and then landed on the wall of the patio, staring at us. Lorena didn't seem to notice. She reached into her purse and pulled out a photograph. "This is why I was late," she said, placing it on the table. "I went home to get this."

It was a picture of a man on a horse. Although I knew nothing about horses, or the people who loved them, I understood immediately that to say this man was "riding" would have been an understatement, even an insult. It was more like the man and this magnificent animal— for I could tell that the horse was like no horse I'd ever seen—were conducting some kind of elaborate dance, a coordinated expression of grace. The horse's front feet were lifted slightly off the ground, which accentuated the muscles of its haunches and shoulders; its coat was a deep chestnut brown and its mane and tail were shiny and black. Looking at the photograph, I could almost see the movement. And moving with it was the man, clad in jeans and a cream-colored button-down shirt, a wide-rimmed cowboy hat. He held the reins with firm but easy strength, and he sat in the saddle as if he'd sprung to life there. He had the same smooth, broad face as Lorena, yet there was an openness to it, an expression of utter joy. This was a man, I thought, who was doing what he was supposed to be doing in life. This was a man whose normal state was motion.

"Your brother?" I asked needlessly.

"Yes. From three years ago. With Alfonso, his favorite horse."

"Does he still have him?"

"*Have* him? Please. Alfonso wasn't his. None of them were. Those horses cost at least a hundred thousand dollars."

I pushed the photograph back over to her, afraid it would get splashed with beer; afraid that if anything happened to it, something else would befall the man it depicted.

"He was the best horse trainer on the Central Coast," she said. "He loved riding horses. Just loved it."

"How did he get into it?" I asked.

Lorena took another drink. "Our father was a ranch hand and we grew up on the Leary ranch. My mother worked for the Learys too, around the house. The family kept cattle but their real love was breeding and training quarter horses. For shows, I mean, not ranch work—for reining competitions, and Jimmy was riding almost before he could walk. I was always bookish—always the nerdy student—but Jimmy couldn't be kept inside."

Another seagull flew overhead, letting out a shrill cry, and this time Lorena looked up. When she lowered her eyes again I saw the sadness there. "He apprenticed with the Learys' trainer and then started to train himself," she continued. "He'd travel with them to shows all over the West—Idaho, Montana, Colorado. Then about five years ago Mr. Leary died, and his son wasn't interested in keeping up the operation. My parents moved into a small place in Paso, and Jimmy started hiring himself out. Then the Larsons found him and brought him on full-time. Charles Larson fancied himself a horseman, and was getting serious about competing. He offered more money than Jimmy could make on his own, even a house on the property. Jimmy and Ana had the kids by then, so it made perfect sense."

And now her eyes filled with tears. One fell, and she angrily wiped it away.

"I'm so sorry about what happened to him," I said. And I was.

"What is it to you?" she demanded. "Why are you here?"

I took a sip of beer, trying to gather my nerve. "It's like I said. Someone down in Los Angeles wants to find out what happened. They've got a sense that maybe things weren't handled the way they should have been."

"Oh really," she said sarcastically. "Do they really? Who the hell is it? Are they connected to the Larsons?"

"No," I said, relieved to be telling the truth. "It's actually a totally uninvolved party. They just want to find out the full story. Make people do the right thing."

"And what would that be, at this point?"

"I don't know." I was treading on dangerous ground, not sure where the land mines were. "You tell me."

She took the glass of beer in her hand but didn't lift it; instead she squeezed it so hard I thought it might break. "You know what would be good? You know what I'd really like? If someone would just do what they're *supposed* to do and punish the person responsible."

"But Charles Larson is dead. His son too."

She looked at me with much the same expression Professor Rose had worn when she returned my chapters with their weak, half-hearted arguments. "Charles Larson was pretty useless, but he wasn't a jerk. He respected my brother. He was good to his kids. And he never would have been driving at high speed, drunk, with his son in the car."

"But . . . but that's what was reported," I sputtered, realizing again that actually *nothing* had been reported. "If Charles Larson wasn't driving, then who was?" Yet even as I asked the question, I thought of what I already knew: the check from Mrs. W—, and the injuries to her son. Those injuries included broken ribs, consistent with what happened when a driver was thrown against a steering wheel.

"Someone who was visiting the Larsons," Lorena said. "Some asshole from Bel Air. I don't know his name. I just know that he nearly killed my brother. And on some days, to tell you the truth, I almost wish he had."

Her eyes filled with tears again, and I looked away, past the edge of the patio, out toward the cars driving by on Moonstone Drive, and at the trees, the beach, the ocean. She didn't know who the other man was. But I did. And it took every bit of self-control I had to keep my composure.

When I trusted myself to speak, I asked, "If people know this, why didn't they tell anyone?"

Lorena took a moment to answer. "I don't know that anyone *does* know, except my brother. He was in a coma for a couple of weeks after the accident, and the other survivor told the police that Charles Larson was driving." She paused, gripping her drink again. "Jimmy told us different, though. He told us the truth: that the other guy was driving, and Charles was too drunk to know what was going on, and Jimmy went with them to try and keep things under control. But when the cops finally questioned him, it was already too late, because by that point the money had come."

I tried not to seem overinterested, though I felt my pulse quicken. "The money?"

"The hush money. The bribe. From the driver, I guess, or his family. I never found out the exact details because I was so disgusted by it. But my parents and Ana decided to take it. In Jimmy's name, through his business."

"His business?"

"His horse-training business. First Quarter."

I held her eyes for a moment, then had to look away. First Quarter. So that's what it was.

"*Think of the care he needs*, they said," Lorena went on. "*Think about the future of his children.* And so both my parents and Ana bought new places in Paso Robles, and Jimmy has a full-time caregiver, and everyone's happy. Except for me. And Jimmy. And of course the Larson family, who still believe that Charles caused the accident."

I took this all in, with a sense that I'd just stepped into a land much vaster and more frightening than I'd imagined. "Couldn't you go to the police?" I asked.

Lorena laughed bitterly. "For what? You don't think that someone who's rich enough to buy off my family has power over them too? And the Larsons—they kept the whole thing out of the paper. They control too much of the business and government around here for anyone to cross them. Suddenly they make big gifts to the Police Protective League, the Fireman's League. So if I go to the police, I'll be laughed at or ignored, and then my family gets cut off from the money. I don't approve of them taking it, but I don't want to be the reason they lose it, either. And so I just keep going on, and mind my own business. And dream about getting out of here."

I just sat there staring at the remnants of my beer, a half-inch of piss-colored liquid. It was a dirty business, what she'd told me, and yet I knew it was true. I thought of Mrs. W—, her haughty carriage and deep pride, and couldn't help but feel differently about her. I thought too of what Fiona would say when I told her that her suspicions had been right. Steven J—, who everyone acknowledged was a ne'er-do-well, had actually done real damage—damage beyond forgiving or repair. And this young woman sitting with me had to bear, along with her grief, the lonely burden of a truth that no one wanted to act on, or even to hear.

We finally left the Sand Bar a little after five thirty, just as it was starting to fill up for dinner. I was supposed to head back to LA, but on a whim I turned left onto the highway and drove farther up the coast. I passed the outer boundaries of Cambria, the few restaurants and private houses. I passed the tacky motels of San Simeon and the driver-trap greasy restaurants. I passed the cove where the elephant seals were sleeping on the beach, dozens of cars expelling tourists to watch them. I drove another fifteen, twenty miles, and when I saw the giant, leaning rock in the water that Lorena had described, I looked to the inland side and, within another mile, saw the driveway that she'd told me to watch for. It was nondescript, not even marked by a number, but paved and clearly cared for. It bent to the right and up a rise so suddenly that you couldn't tell where it went. I drove on for another half-mile, and found the turnoff that Lorena had mentioned, a gravel cutout on the ocean side of the road. I got out of the car and stared back across the highway.

The Larsons owned something like twenty thousand acres, and I was probably seeing just a couple hundred of them. It was beautiful land, the small steep bluff at the bottom giving way to gentle rolling slopes, and beyond that a broad expanse of lush green mountain. A few low clouds hung over the land, obscuring the gentle peaks. I stood there, the ocean crashing below me, feeling the wind at my back, and stared up at this wild, pristine piece of California; it seemed odd that anyone could claim it was theirs. And yet the Larson family owned this land, and had owned it for decades. Somewhere up there, above the clouds, was a mansion whose grandiosity was beyond imagining. And below it, on the gentler terrain closer to the road, was the airstrip where Jimmy Castillo had been horribly injured; where Charles Larson and his son had died. It seemed unreal that something so tragic and avoidable had occurred in this grand, gorgeous place. But it had, at the cost of men's futures and lives, and the costs were still being exacted. I stared up at the hills for another fifteen or twenty minutes, but I saw no sign of the house or human activity. The land would not yield its secrets. So I got back into my car and headed home.

I wish I could say that I thought about Jimmy Castillo on my drive back to Los Angeles. I wish I could say I considered his family—his wife and children, his heartbroken parents, his tough, pained sister. This is what I'd rather believe of myself: that when I learned the actual story of the accident and the death and grief it had caused, when I understood who was really responsible, I empathized with the Castillos—as well as the Larsons—and felt a deep, healthy anger at Steven J— for his stupidity and carelessness. But that wasn't where my head was, or more truthfully, my heart. That would have been giving myself too much credit.

What I really thought about was Fiona. I pictured her face when I revealed what I'd learned; how she'd throw her arms around me, grateful and impressed. I saw us leaning our heads together, coconspirators. And as the winding two-lane highway curved in from the ocean and met up with the 101, my hopes ventured further, onto my life and hers, and how they might intertwine.

The first thing I had to do was change my career. There was no way a woman like Fiona would be satisfied with a mere academic, and truth be told, my studies were feeling musty and useless. I needed a career that placed me in the world of tangible accomplishment;

that allowed me a sizable living; that gave me entrée to mingle with the kinds of women and men who made up Fiona's world. And shifting gears in this way might also make me able—at last—to provide some support for my family. I swung back and forth between business and law; from the time I left San Luis Obispo until I hit Santa Barbara, I had changed my mind three or four times. But by then I had a general plan. I'd drop out of the history program, and enter business or law school; between student loans and the assistance that Mrs. W— had offered, I could find a way to swing the tuition. It's some measure of my delusion that this plan depended on the help of the woman I was about to betray.

The rest of it was tricky, since Fiona had a family. But clearly she wasn't in love with her husband. She'd have to leave him, maybe not immediately, but sometime soon, and it would be messy for a while, but that would pass. Her family money would ensure that she'd be all right financially, and then we would be free. And her son—although she rarely mentioned him, I'm sure she'd want custody. That was fine—I'd always wanted kids, and as I contemplated living with a six-year-old, I felt a little jolt of excitement at remembering she was still young enough to have another child. I imagined taking her to meet my family, how reserved and suspicious my mother would act before she warmed up; how dazzled my father would be. I imagined walking on the beach with her, hand in hand; I imagined leisurely mornings in bed. I imagined all sorts of things on that long, late night, driving through the dark to Los Angeles.

I waited until morning to call her. When I finally did,

around ten, she told me to come to her house—everyone was gone, and her housekeeper was off that day. She lived in a white Colonial in the flatlands of Beverly Hills—a large home to be sure, but not as outsized as some I'd seen, and this comforted me somehow, made her and a possible life with her seem less out of reach. She opened the door as I was coming up the walkway, and as I took in the vision of her, in another pastel dress, I looked forward to a lifetime of moments like this, me coming home, her greeting me at the doorway. She pulled me inside and shut the door and gave me a long, slow kiss.

"I've missed you," she said.

"I've missed you too," I answered. And everything— the trip, the expense, the digging up of information— was worth it.

She took my hand and pulled me into the house, so fast I could barely glance at the space around me. In a short hallway there were photographs, only one of which I got a good look at—a school picture of a young, dark-haired boy who must have been her son, in a jacket and tie, looking out at the camera with a polite, subdued expression. His image stayed with me as we entered the bright kitchen. I don't think I'd quite believed he was real.

The kitchen was larger than my living room, a light-filled, expansive space that actually felt used and lived in. Fiona led me to a chair at a large wood-and-steel table and poured us both some coffee. She sat at the end, perpendicular to me, close enough to touch, and I told her what I had found. When I described the young man in the restaurant reacting to Jimmy Castillo's name, her lips parted slightly; when I related the moment of first seeing Jimmy's sister, she sat up in anticipation. And when I told her what Lorena had revealed to me, that Steven J— had been the driver, she thumped her fist on the table and exclaimed, "I *knew* it!" Her eyes were churning with what I took to be the satisfaction of solving a puzzle. But I didn't have time to think about it because she got up, shoved my chair back, and straddled me, and all thoughts of accidents and secrets escaped me.

She unbuckled my belt and unzipped my pants, shoving them down just far enough to pull me out of them. She wasn't wearing panties, and when she ground down against me, I thrust myself inside her. We grasped and bucked together, urgent and strong, and she pulled my hair so hard I was sure she'd come away with a handful. I picked her up, still inside her, and laid her down on the table, pushing the cups aside and barely noticing when they crashed to the floor. She pulled me into her and exhorted me, harder, harder; reached up and wrapped her hands around my throat. The sounds that came out of her were deep, primal sounds, and her eyes were filled with fire. I felt something like an earthquake inside of me, a fundamental shattering. This was totally different—not only from our first time together, but from any sex I'd ever experienced. I hadn't known that Fiona was capable of such urgency, such passion. And I was naïve and enraptured and stupid enough to believe it was directed at me.

CHAPTER NINE

The next Monday, I drove up to Mrs. W—'s estate. It had been a week since I was last there—I'd taken Tuesday off to go up to Cambria, and then Lourdes had called Friday morning to say that Mrs. W— couldn't see me that day. Although I'd tried to put it out of my mind, I was feeling increasingly guilty about what I'd taken off to do, and worse about what I'd discovered. I tried to justify this by telling myself I'd had no idea what I would find. Besides, Fiona and I weren't going to *do* anything with the information about Steven J—. It was just interesting to have. Yet the truth was, I felt shitty. Whatever Mrs. W— had done to cover up for her son's actions, she'd been generous, even caring, with me.

When I knocked on the door, no one answered. As I stood on the doorstep, looking out at the property, I noticed that it was strangely quiet. No one was taking care of the plants or lugging food for the animals. There were no voices or laughter coming out of the garage, where often someone was tending to the cars. This was strange—was everyone off today? I knocked one more time, and finally the door was pulled open. But instead of Lourdes I was greeted by an unfamiliar middle-aged man, who considered me suspiciously. "Can I help you?"

"I'm Richard Nagano," I said. "I'm here to see Mrs. W—. Is she around? Or Lourdes?"

The man looked me up and down, as if trying to figure out my scam. "They're not here," he said. "I'm Bart J—. Marion's son."

I looked at him more closely now, and recognized the man from his picture. He was probably fifty, but looked older. His thick hair was almost entirely gray, and his skin was sun-darkened and ruddy. But he had the high, prominent cheeks of his mother, the same firm and steady jaw. He wore jeans, a blue plaid shirt, and work boots, and although his head was bare, I could envision the cowboy hat that I knew was usually affixed there; I discerned a faint line across his forehead.

"I've been doing some work for your mother," I explained. "I'm a graduate student at USC, and she hired me for a project."

Now a light of recognition came to his face. "Oh, oh, yes. I know who you are. I'm sorry. Nice to meet you, Richard." With that he extended his hand, and I shook it. His grip was firm and his skin work-toughened. "My mother's in the hospital."

"*What?*"

He lifted his hand as if holding me back. "She's okay. Or she will be. She has a heart condition, and sometimes it weakens her enough that she has to be hospitalized. I'm sorry, Lourdes did mention that this was one of your days. I just forgot to call you."

With that he ushered me in, took me into the dining room, and brought us both glasses of water. The two Lhasa apsos circled our legs, hopeful and confused. I noticed, with a pang, that the framed picture of the dogs in their wine-bottle costumes—which I'd brought a couple of weeks before—was sitting on the cabinet.

"How long has she been in the hospital?" I asked when he sat down, feeling terrible that I hadn't known.

"Since Thursday. Lourdes called the paramedics when she was having trouble breathing. This happens every once in a while, and I keep telling her she needs a live-in nurse. But she refuses the help. She's a tough old woman," he said, with clear admiration.

Thursday. On Thursday I'd gone to Fiona's house, and we'd had sex in the kitchen. That day I hadn't even thought about Mrs. W—.

"She's coming home tomorrow," Bart continued. "She's determined to be fully recovered by the Founders' Luncheon. You should stop by, she'd be happy to see you. I know how much she's enjoyed your company."

I took all of this in without comment; I don't think I could have felt any worse than I did. "Well, I enjoy her company too," I said finally.

"This project of hers . . . I'm sure it's worthwhile, but it's caused her stress too. She's trying to finish it now because she thinks she's dying."

I gulped and held myself steady. "Is she?"

"I don't think so, but no one knows when it comes to the heart. I get the sense she thinks she's living on borrowed time. Anyway," he said, more brightly now, "thank you for spending time with her. She gets lonely, you know. And I don't get down here nearly as often as I should."

"The project's almost done," I assured him. "And it really has been wonderful to work with her. I've learned so much." I paused. "She must be thrilled you're here. It's got to be tough for you to leave your ranch, I imagine. And don't you do a cattle run or something about now?"

He cocked his head, surprised, and gave a broad smile; I could see the genuine warmth there. "Actually, it's not for another couple of months. But my mother told you that? She doesn't usually deign to discuss my work. She wishes I'd trade in my ranch clothes for a tuxedo and expensive shoes. Thinks I should be doing something that doesn't involve horse manure and cow pies."

"I'm not sure she did tell me," I said, trying to remember. "It could have been Lourdes. Or Fiona."

"Fiona?" He sounded surprised. "Fiona Harrington?"

"Yes," I said after recalling her maiden name. "Fiona Morgan now. I've gotten to know her a bit, through events I've gone to with your mother. It sounds like you know her too?"

"You could say that. She was engaged to my brother."

I had brought the glass of water up to my mouth but now my throat clenched tight. My hand was shaking as I lowered it back to the table. "She was *what*?"

"She was engaged to my brother Steven. For five or six years. He destroyed their relationship, as is his fashion, in spectacular style."

My heart, which had been riding up in my chest for days, almost shot up through my throat. It was a warm day, but a chill shook my body. "She never mentioned that," I managed feebly.

Bart sighed and laid one weathered hand on the table. "It doesn't surprise me. She was humiliated. Steven drank and played around, and it all came to a head when he brought another woman to a wedding. *That's* how he broke it off with her, by parading a new girlfriend—and *girlfriend* is being generous—in front of all their friends.

My mother was furious—she liked Fiona, but even more, she was enraged at how Steven's behavior reflected on the family. She won't let anyone talk about it, even now. Steven married a completely different girl a few months later, and then divorced her to marry another. I'm not even sure who he's with now, or what he's up to—he was involved in a bad accident a couple of years ago and he pretty much stopped talking to us all." He paused, and I wondered what he knew or didn't know about the circumstances of the accident. "But we were all so glad for Fiona when she married Aaron Morgan, who's a straight shooter, and successful, and very good to her, I hear. A much better man, sadly, than my brother."

As Bart talked, I felt myself shrinking. The room simultaneously expanded and started to spin. The significance and magnitude of my time with Fiona, of the events of the last few months, bore down on me and ground me into nothing. She hadn't wanted to know about the accident at Cliffhaven, I realized now, out of simple, prurient curiosity. She'd wanted to know because she had something at stake. Fiona needed information on Steven, and now she had it. Thanks to me.

I realized how convenient I must have been for her— how useful my access to Mrs. W—and her house. I realized how easy I'd been to play. She'd been so brazen— pushing me to get what she needed, trusting that the shame of Mrs. W—, and the code of silence amongst her peers, would keep me in the dark about her past. As this understanding came over me in waves, I felt a welling anger, and shame, and finally horror, at what I'd allowed myself to be party to. No, not party to; it wasn't that passive—in what I had done of my own free will.

"How long ago did all of this happen?"

"Oh, maybe nine, ten years ago," Bart said, waving it off. "It's ancient history now."

I couldn't meet his eyes, and so I turned out toward the entrance hall, where the painting of the maze looked bright and green in the late-morning sun. The boy lingered as always toward the edge of the maze; the girl was ensconced in the middle. But gazing at the picture now, in this light and from this angle, I noticed that the path the boy was on never actually led to the center. The neat trim of the shrubs and the beauty of the landscape made the center seem accessible, but the path circled and led back out of the maze. There was no way the boy would ever get to the girl. He would wander in circles, the girl visible, tempting, but always just out of his reach.

Later, much later, I'd learn more about Fiona and Steven. How they had known each other since they were children; how their grandfathers, who'd been business partners, had practically promised them to one another. They'd each been raised appropriately in their separate, gendered spheres—he attending Harvard-Westlake when it was still a boys' school, she attending Marlborough. They saw each other regularly at family events; at the Colonial Club and various weddings—always with other people around, always chaperoned. They were allowed—even encouraged—to date other people, with the understanding that it was all rehearsal for their eventual bonding. Finally, after Steven graduated from Stanford Business School and Fiona from Wellesley, their formal courtship had begun. They'd dated for a year before they got engaged, and then—breaking with protocol—they decided to live together, buying a condominium in Pacific Palisades while they both established their careers. Neither Fiona's parents nor Mrs. W— were happy with this arrangement, yet they put aside their disapproval in light of the obvious larger good— the planned union of two of the city's most illustrious families; the perpetuation of their influence and wealth.

But then trouble started, first Steven's travails at his brokerage house, then his drinking; it was not clear which was the cause and which the result. He started to disappear on days-long benders and was seen with other women, including the high-end prostitute with whom he was famously caught at the after-hours club. The collectors of gossip did not record how Fiona responded, but there were accounts of her being subdued and quiet, of unexplained bruises, and suggestions of discord, maybe violence. All of this was swept aside, though, when they announced a wedding date; there was a notice of their engagement, I found later, in the *Beverly Hills Courier*, a local weekly I'd never thought to look at. But then came the friend's wedding that Bart had referred to, involving another society family. Steven had gone missing from the condo he shared with Fiona, probably on another bender. So she'd attended the wedding solo, where she ran into Steven, who was drunk and unshaven, accompanied by an underage girl rumored to be yet another prostitute. Stunned and heartbroken, Fiona had tried to avoid a scene, but he'd yelled at her during the reception, thrown a glass or two, announced that he'd rather sleep with a new whore every night than spend another evening with a frigid bitch like her.

Steven was sent to a dry-out facility at the behest of his mother, who also cut off access to his trust; she must have compensated for her own embarrassment by coming down on him with swift, public harshness. She paid Fiona for Steven's share of their condo, and with that, the ties between the families were broken. Fiona had been twenty-eight when the engagement fell apart; Steven was thirty-four. She disappeared from view for more than a year, Bart later told me, and when she reemerged, she was engaged to Aaron Morgan.

This was the story I eventually heard; this was what happened almost a decade before I first drove to Mrs. W—'s gate. But I knew none of it when I went to see Fiona the following day, wanting, hoping for some different explanation.

I'd texted her as soon as I'd driven down the hill after talking with Bart, writing simply, *I need to talk to you.* But maybe she sensed my distress, or maybe she understood that the game was up, because she didn't reply, to that first text or to the six or seven others that followed.

By evening I understood that I wasn't going to hear from her, and so early the next morning I drove to Beverly Hills and parked my car across the street from her house. It was seven forty a.m., but I knew her husband had already left for work. At seven fifty, a woman I didn't know—probably the nanny or housekeeper—emerged from the front door with a boy in tow. He was a gangly thing, brown-haired and awkward, but unconsciously handsome, with an air of decency and sweetness that I immediately understood must have been inherited from his father. I saw the sharp angles of Fiona's jaw line, the fineness of his rosy skin. I saw him look up at the woman with uncertain, hopeful eyes, and I felt a pang of sadness for this boy, who brought no joy to his mother; who had done nothing wrong besides get himself fathered by a man who was not the man his mother still loved.

When they had driven off, I got out of the car and knocked on the front door. For a moment I wondered what would happen if someone other than Fiona answered; then I realized I didn't really care. After a second knock Fiona pulled the door open. She was wearing a crisp gray suit, and her face was rigid, impenetrable.

"I can't see you right now, Richard. I'm already late."

I raised my hand to keep her from shutting the door in my face. "You didn't tell me that you were *engaged* to Steven."

For a moment a flash of guilt came over her face, but it was quickly subsumed by something slyer and colder. "You never asked," she said. "You never asked how I knew him."

"Don't you think that might have been useful for me to know?"

"Why? What good would it have done?"

"What good? No good, I guess, except it would have explained why you were so damned *interested* in what he was up to. It might have given me second thoughts about what I was doing."

"Oh, please," she said disdainfully. "It's not like I forced you. You were *eager* to help. Besides, what are you complaining about? You got what you wanted."

This was a kick in the gut, and I looked at her incredulously. But the face of the woman before me was so different from the smiling and encouraging face I'd known over the last several months that I might have been confronting a stranger. I wanted to say, *You took advantage of me, you played on my emotions.* But she was right—I wasn't some innocent boy; I'd gone along with her happily, willingly.

And now her face darkened even more. "Besides, you did something useful, Richard. That man is a *monster*. He throws his money and his cars around and smashes everything in his path. Steven *destroyed* me, and then he destroyed Charlie Larson and his son, and he always seems to weasel out of it. But there's no getting out of this one—I'm going to make sure that people know what he did. I'm going to make sure that he's ruined!"

"Why the hell would you *do* that? I understand that he hurt you. I get it. But why would you want to do that to Mrs. W—?"

"Oh, please," she said again. "She's as bad as he is."

"I don't believe that," I said. And I didn't. I just then realized I didn't.

Something shifted in Fiona's eyes; it was like the crust of the earth had opened and I could see the roiling inferno beneath. "You say he hurt me. Yes, he *hurt* me, all right. He abused and humiliated me and laughed when I cried. You don't think he learned that from somewhere? You think he was just *born* evil? That Marion didn't have any effect on shaping who he became?" She paused and her expression grew more bitter and cold. "I *hate* that man," she spat out. "You have no idea, Richard. You have no idea how much I've suffered."

I heard the depth of the anger in her voice; I saw the twisted look of vindication. I understood that this rage was more entrenched and real than the facts of her present life.

"I feel bad for you, Fiona," I said. And I didn't mean about Steven. She must have realized that, because she drew herself up to her full height now, into the comfort of her wealth and history.

"*You* feel bad for *me*?"

She was right, of course. She was going to be fine. She always would be, no matter how much she claimed to suffer. But then I thought of Charles Larson and his son, of his wife and grieving parents. I thought of Jimmy Castillo and his family, his unbendable sister, and of how Fiona hadn't even mentioned them in her account of lives destroyed. I shook my head, disgusted with both of us, and turned and walked away from the house.

CHAPTER TEN

The USC Founders' Luncheon where Mrs. W—
was being honored took place on the second
Tuesday in May, Mrs. W—'s actual birthday. Because it was a milestone birthday—seventy-five—and
because Mrs. W—, for once, was giving a gift that bore
her name, it was a particularly illustrious affair. Mrs.
W— pretended not to care about it, but it was clear
that she did; she'd brought it up often as the day approached, wondering who would come, and what outfit
she should wear.

I'd spent the last two weeks waiting anxiously for
something to happen—a piece in the paper maybe, or an
unexpected call to Mrs. W—. I couldn't anticipate what
Fiona would do, though I saw her clearly enough now
to know she'd do something. She'd carried her grudge
for far too long to be satisfied by keeping her hard-won
information to herself.

During this period I went up to Mrs. W—'s house a
half a dozen times. She'd come back from the hospital
the day after I met Bart, and waved off any attempt to
discuss her health or offer sympathy. My transcription of
her journals was almost complete, ending with her story
of Langley W—: his early years in New Hampshire, his
move to the West, the triumphs and travails of his business. Some of it was consistent with the remembrances

of the Colonial Club; much of it was totally different. Reading this account, I knew I'd been given a view into history that no one else outside the family would ever see. But whatever pleasure I might have had in this privilege, or in being in that storied house, was gone; it was tainted now, and I had done the tainting. Even the knowledge that she'd let an innocent man take the blame for his own death—the awareness of her manipulation and dishonesty—could not overcome my sense of guilt. I couldn't bring myself to tell Mrs. W— about what had happened, yet I couldn't make myself leave her, either. I moved through the great front entryway and high-ceilinged rooms with the sense I was already a ghost.

On the day of the luncheon, as was our custom, I drove up to her place so that Dalton could take us down together. When I arrived, I slipped off to the room where I'd worked the last few months, came back, and presented Mrs. W— with a wrapped package. I placed it on the dining room table, which was decorated with bouquets of flowers and baskets of goodies from Jessica, Bart, and several entities with whom she did business. I felt a twinge of sadness that her children weren't there— Jessica would never participate in such events, I'd come to learn; Bart sent what seemed to be honest regrets.

"What is this?" she asked, almost suspiciously.

"Open it."

She sat down and pulled the paper apart, confused even when she saw the brown ring binder inside, until she opened it and looked at the pages.

"It's all there," I explained. "Your entire journal. Eight hundred and twenty-seven typed pages."

Her mouth opened slightly as she flipped through the pages—she looked like she was in disbelief.

"I know you'll want a fancier binding," I said. "But I thought you'd enjoy seeing it all printed out." It was not an elaborate presentation, to be sure—I'd bought the nicest binder I could find in an art supply store, used the printer in the office, and snuck a hole puncher in to punch and bind the pages. But from Mrs. W—'s expression, you'd have thought I'd presented her with a rare first edition, some treasure that had long been thought lost.

"Thank you, Richard." She smiled and stood up, and then gave a polite, formal bow. "Thank you very much."

Dalton drove us down to the Ludlow Hotel, where the luncheon was taking place. It was relatively small for this type of affair, about two hundred people—but that seemed appropriate for what was essentially a public birthday party. All of Mrs. W—'s friends and acquaintances were there—Betty Baker, the Delaneys, the Westbrooks, the Bestharts—representatives from LA's most important families. Caroline Randall, whose house I'd gone to in Beverly Park, came over and gave Mrs. W— a genuine, smiling embrace. I saw Fiona's mother out of the corner of my eye, and I knew Fiona would be arriving soon too.

Mrs. W— looked amazing, of course; she wore an emerald-gray long jacket with some kind of peach-colored sash, over smooth gray dress pants. Her hair was perfectly arranged in curls that framed her face. There were journalists from all the major fashion and society magazines—*Town & Country*, *Vanity Fair*, *W*, *Angelino*, *Vogue*—and everyone wanted to photograph her, so she spent almost twenty minutes at the step-and-repeat. *Town & Country* was doing an entire spread on her, for what was apparently the third time.

We made our way to the head table, where everyone was polite enough not to mention the absence of her children. We were seated with several of Mrs. W—'s oldest friends—Betty Baker, Lydia Fehringer, Margaret Delaney—as well as the head of the USC Medical Center—the recipient of her gift—and the president of the university. It was a little heady for me to be seated with him, especially when Mrs. W— began to tell him what an exceptional talent I was and how the school would be lucky to have me in its law or business school. "If you like having my donation," she said to him, "you will make sure that this young man is accepted." I picked nervously at the preset salad, and a plate of miso-glazed salmon with quinoa was served in quick order. Chef François DeLorme had catered, and he came out himself to present Mrs. W— with a chocolate birthday cake, ceremonious and smiling. If he remembered me from the luncheon in Beverly Park, he didn't show it.

The formal program began as soon as dessert was served—the president of the Founders' Club welcomed the crowd and talked about the hospital, and about what Mrs. W—'s gift would mean for its research and treatment efforts. Then Mrs. W—'s longtime acquaintance Hattie Clark took the stage and introduced a slide show of Mrs. W—'s life. There were photographs of Mrs. W— as a young girl, with her grandfather; in one, they sat happily on a staircase surrounded by three Brittany spaniels. There was a picture of her on a horse, carrying a shotgun. There were photos of her in her twenties and thirties, wearing elaborate gowns; and other pictures from later, where she was in more reserved suits, at openings and groundbreakings. There was a picture of her in perhaps her late twenties, dancing with a dark-haired tuxedoed man whose image I hadn't seen before. She leaned over and whispered, "That's Baron, right after we were married. He was my dreamboat." There was a shot of her maybe a decade later, on a clay court in tennis whites; and another in which she wore an old-fashioned one-piece bathing suit with a skirt and posed at Santa Monica Beach. And then an image of her in her thirties with her three small children, who ranged, it looked, between two and eight. Bart already had a frank, practical expression, and Jessica looked like any normal four- or five-year-old girl with ribbons and curls. But Steven, who was just a baby, was staring off camera almost spacily, as if his attention had already wandered.

Except for the photograph of her children, during which she tensed, Mrs. W— seemed to enjoy the display immensely. She kept commenting on where this or that picture was taken, which was fun for me too, since I knew so many of the places and players from her journal. The audience laughed at some of the more amusing shots—like one of her and her girlfriends dressed up as lady vampires for Halloween—and there were sounds of recognition and remembrance. It was a wonderful tribute, and when the lights went back up, I helped Mrs. W— to the front, where a bulky, suited Ludlow staffer offered his arm and escorted her up to the stage.

She did not approach the microphone—she disliked public speaking—but stood beside the podium as the head of the Founders' Club handed her a crystal award.

The audience clapped politely, and there was even a single "Yes!" shouted enthusiastically by a young male designer, perhaps a previous walker. Mrs. W— nodded to acknowledge the applause, and smiled for a photograph, then quickly made her way off the stage. I went to retrieve her again, and as she reengaged my arm, I felt the joy in her grasp.

But I couldn't shake the sense that something was off, and I'd felt it as soon as we arrived. People were somehow reserved—not the usual politeness because of Mrs. W—'s standing, but something else, a holding back, an assessment. The women who usually clamored to be photographed with her seemed to hesitate this time; I saw several people notice us and turn away. Her tablemates were less effusive than usual, and as the slide show played, I'd felt a kind of questioning, of judgment. And there was no mistaking the titter that had gone through the crowd when the picture of her children was shown.

When Mrs. W— was seated again, I excused myself and found my way to the restroom. Since the men's room was past the women's, and the women's inevitably had a line, I overheard the women standing outside the door and even—when the door opened—some conversation from within.

"Can you believe," I heard someone say, "that they'd actually show a *picture* of that man?"

"She always did clean up after him," said someone else. "I guess it's no different this time."

"But poor Marjory," came a third voice as the door was swinging closed. "To think that for two years Marion let her believe it was Charles . . ."

I froze. Were they talking about what I thought they were talking about? It couldn't be. But then the door swung open again and somebody said, ". . . to think it was *Steven* who survived." And I knew that it was.

I felt my face flush. My heart began to pound, and I had the sensation that my anger and incredulity were making my hair stand on end. Of course this was what Fiona would do. She would never, as I'd feared, give a tip to the papers; she didn't care about conventional publicity. And she would never confront Mrs. W— directly; that was not her style, and besides, what could Mrs. W— do for her? No, what mattered to Fiona was what their own friends thought—their reputations in society. And that mattered to Mrs. W— too. The worst thing Fiona could do, I understood, was reveal what Steven—and his mother—had done, to the people within their own circle. And so she'd engaged in a whisper campaign, planting a seed of gossip here, a tidbit there. She probably told a few key friends—demanding their secrecy, of course— and then waited for human nature to work.

I managed to get in and out of the restroom, checking the mirror to make sure I was presentable. By the time I got back to the ballroom, it was already half-empty— and the weird pall over the crowd, their hurry to leave, just confirmed what I already suspected.

I made my way through the current of departing women like a salmon fighting its way upstream. And at the end of it, waiting for the crowd to dissipate, I found Fiona, sitting alone at a table and calmly reapplying her lipstick.

"You had to tell people, didn't you?" I accused. "And you couldn't have waited, at least until after today?"

Fiona looked up at me impassively. This made my pulse jump: despite everything, she was still beautiful to me, and the exorcising of her rage only made her more so. "I don't know what you're talking about," she said.

"Oh bullshit," I responded, my voice a bit too loud. "I know what you've done. I heard people *talking* about it."

Fiona stood up and faced me directly. She looked half-bored, half-amused. "If you're referring to the accident, well then, yes, I may have mentioned to Marjory Larson that her son had been unfairly blamed for the accident. I may have mentioned it to Charles's wife too. I thought they deserved to know."

I was breathing hard, as if I'd just run up a flight of stairs. She was right—they *did* have a right to know. But so much else about this was wrong, and in my jumble of confusion, all I could do for a moment was shake my head and glare. "That's not *all* you told them, though, is it? You told them about Mrs. W—."

She smiled. "Well, that *is* a rather integral part of the story."

"And they're not the only ones you told, either. Other people seem to know."

Fiona laughed, a sound without mirth. "I may have mentioned it to one or two of my closest friends. But what happened after that, Richard, is out of my control."

I just stared at her, finally taking a couple of steps back to try to control my anger. "You're disgusting," I said. "And to think that I ever . . ."

"Wanted me? Jumped at the chance to fuck me? Thought that I gave a shit about you? Well, that was *your* mistake, darling. You believed what you chose to believe."

"What's going on here?"

Both Fiona and I turned to find Mrs. W— standing ten feet away. Almost all of the guests had filtered out, and only the hotel staff, clearing plates away, remained. She had made her way over to us, leaning on her cane; now she stood looking at us, concerned.

I felt like a kid caught in a school-yard fight, yet I was so angry that I couldn't think or speak coherently. *She did wrong*, I wanted to say, and that's essentially what I did say: "Why don't you tell her, Fiona? Why don't you tell her what you've done?"

Fiona's expression changed from that of a caught child to something more complex and self-satisfied. She had no reason to fear Mrs. W— anymore, and she knew it; she held the upper hand. "I've just happened to get some interesting information, Marion. Information about your son."

Mrs. W— looked at her, impatient, annoyed.

"I know it was Steven who caused the accident at Cliffhaven. And I know you paid off the other survivor."

Mrs. W—'s expression didn't change, and Fiona flushed and went on: "You and Steven have let everyone believe that Charles Larson was driving. But now I know the truth, Marion. I know what you and Steven have done!"

Her voice wavered at the end, sounding triumphant, a bit hysterical. But if Fiona expected Mrs. W— to react with shame or fear, she must have been sorely disappointed. Mrs. W— just continued to look at her—calm, unmovable. "Yes," she said. "What of it?"

Fiona stared at her, incredulous. "What *of* it? Your son *killed* people, Marion. He killed one of *us*! And you used your money to get him out of it, and to silence the only other witness."

Mrs. W— looked at her with the same measured expression. "I tried to compensate a family who was hurt by his actions," she said calmly. "And as for the money to Steven, that wasn't to help him. That was to make sure he stayed away. To make sure he had enough that there would never be a reason to ask anything of me again."

"What about the Larsons? What about compensating them for how *they* were hurt by his actions?"

"They don't need money," Mrs. W— said. "Besides, there's nothing that can bring Charles and his son back."

"Oh, you're *unbelievable*." Fiona leaned forward and clenched her fists; for a moment I thought she would attack Mrs. W—. "You're just as arrogant as Steven. Well, I'm not just going to sit with this, Marion. I'm going to make sure that everyone knows!"

And now Mrs. W— did something unexpected. She laughed. It was not a bitter laugh, or even an unhappy one. It was a laugh of some belief or suspicion being confirmed; a laugh of someone who was untouchable. "Go ahead, foolish girl. Tell everyone. What do you think you'll accomplish? That you'll reveal that my son is worthless? Well, everybody already knows that. That I gave money to the family of a poor crippled man? They are grateful for the help. All I should have done differently is apologize to the Larsons—you're right—and I will do so today, as soon as I get home. So yes, go ahead, Fiona. Tell whomever you want. All you'll reveal is your own desperation."

Fiona stood there speechless, fuming; she looked like she might combust. For Mrs. W— was right. Even this horrible truth about her son, about her own efforts to protect their name, would—with the right set of actions and the passage of time—fade away into a mildly interesting story that people might or might not remember. The more telling aspect of it all was Fiona's own resentment, which she had nurtured for nearly a decade—and which, it turned out, wasn't entirely spent.

"Let's go, Richard," Mrs. W— said, and I stepped forward to join her.

"You should be careful, Marion," Fiona said now, her voice thin with anger, "about who you let into your house."

Mrs. W— ignored her and I kept closing the space between us.

"How do you think I found out about Steven?" Fiona continued. "I didn't do this on my own—I had help. The help of a very skilled researcher, who had access to your records."

And now, finally, Mrs. W— reacted. She looked at Fiona, who was wearing an ugly smirk, and then turned and searched my face. And what she saw there must have told her that what Fiona said was true. Her mouth opened slightly, and she took an almost imperceptible step backward, as if hit by an invisible blow. The color rose in her cheeks and her eyes appeared brighter. I saw the tiny tremors of disbelief and anger pass over her face; I saw her control and contain them. She lifted her cane an inch or two and then placed it back down, as if unsure what to do with her body. But when she spoke, turning away from me, she looked impenetrable and beautiful, and her voice was clear and strong. "I think you'd better leave now," she said.

I started to reply, to try to defend myself, but she lifted a hand to stop me, still facing away, as if the mere sight of me would cause her harm. I knew I could not reach her, and I couldn't bear to look at Fiona. Already they both seemed very far away. I lowered my head and said, "I'm sorry, Mrs. W—." Then I turned and walked out of the hotel.

CHAPTER ELEVEN

Eighteen months later, I remember the rest of that day with the clarity of some inescapable nightmare. When I emerged from the Ludlow, blinking in the too-bright light, I realized that my car was still at Mrs. W—'s. I did not have the patience to flag down a taxi, so I walked all the way home to Jefferson Park, a distance of about six miles. It took me almost two hours, and I was slowed the last few miles by the blisters that were forming from my dress shoes. But I didn't go into a drugstore to buy Band-Aids; I didn't even stop to rest. The shoes cut and chafed through my thin cotton socks, yet I welcomed the pain. I deserved it.

By the time I rounded the final corner to get to my building, my car was already parked in front. Tucked under one of the wiper blades was a yellow carbon receipt. The car had been towed there, arranged by the sender. A note indicated that my landlord had signed for it.

Not long after I went inside, someone buzzed at the gate, and it was a messenger, bearing a package from Mrs. W—. It contained the few personal items I'd left at her house—a couple of pens, a notebook, a sweater. Included without comment was my final paycheck—to which she'd added a thousand dollars. I half-resented the gesture—it felt like a kiss-off—but I needed the money. I knew I would cash it.

At the very bottom of the package was the picture of the dogs, Pinot and Chardonnay, the frame wrapped in their wine-bottle costumes. I laughed when I saw this, and then the pain hit my gut, and once my tears began, I couldn't stop them. Mrs. W—, for all her complexities, had given me so much, taught me more than I could have imagined. Those silly costumes were the only things I'd ever given her. Of course she was angry with me, but sending the picture and costumes back seemed unnecessary. I thought she was just being punitive, spiteful. It didn't occur to me until much later that I'd broken her heart.

I spent the long, unbearable months of summer in a haze of regret. I tried to get back to work on my dissertation— the real one—but my mind kept wandering to luncheons and glamorous evenings; to Fiona Morgan's face; to the quiet grandiosity of Mrs. W—'s mansion. It seemed implausible that I had ever experienced such things; after a week or two it was hard to believe they'd been real.

In mid-August, I decided to give up on my dissertation—I just didn't care about it anymore. Once I knew for sure that my writing efforts were over, I made two difficult but necessary phone calls: I informed Professor Rose that I was dropping out of the PhD program, and I told the Blain Foundation I was renouncing their funding. It was more than a bit scary to know I was giving up my livelihood, but it didn't feel right to accept the money. Besides, I wanted to be free of it all—I no longer wanted the weight of expectation.

Luckily a few classes opened up at USC, and so I taught a couple of intro history courses. It wasn't much money, but I enjoyed the feeling of earning it, and it was good for me to get out of the house and interact with students; it helped me forget my own troubles. I took in a roommate out of necessity—Corey, a friend of Kevin's, a guy from the fiscal side of the fire department. The four of us spent quite a bit of time together, barbecuing and watching ball games, sitting out on Kevin and Rosanna's patio until late in the evening, laughing until our landlord asked to us to please keep it down. It had been a long time, I realized, since I had laughed like that.

The next spring I applied for a bunch of jobs, mostly with research firms and think tanks, a couple of education-related nonprofits. When I had something solid, I told myself, when I was onto a respectable career, then I'd reconnect with my family. I reached the point of second interviews with the Stanley Research Group and the Student History Project. In both cases, the enthusiasm of the executive directors led me to believe that an offer was imminent, save for a few formalities. But then weeks of silence, and when I called to inquire, some nervous assistant informed me that they had gone with someone else. Was there any feedback? I asked. It would help me with future applications. No, one of the assistants said, just some further information that had come to light. I couldn't imagine what information they meant. Then, on a whim, I looked more closely at both organization's websites, their annual reports and 990 tax forms. Both places received funding from the Harrington Foundation. It turned out that Fiona's reach continued to affect me long after I'd last seen her in person.

I sent out thirty, forty job applications, with discouraging results. Finally, one of my old mentors at USC, who was now a dean at Pasadena City College, offered me a teaching position.

I've just finished my first semester there, teaching four classes, busier than I ever was as a graduate student. It's a lot of work, for not much money, and the junior college students are less prepared than the kids at USC. But I like them better. They're the first in their families to make it past high school; they're the children of gardeners and housekeepers, of welders and garbage collectors, of civil servants and secretaries. They're hardworking and polite and take nothing for granted, and my work with them actually means something. I try to teach them what they need to know about the history of California. I don't tell them that most of the real stories have never been captured in books.

A few months after that last scene at the Ludlow, I wrote Mrs. W— a letter. It was an unforgivable delay, I knew, but it had taken me that long to get my head around all that had happened. I apologized for having violated her trust. I told her how deeply I admired her, how grateful I was for all she'd done for me, how much I'd truly valued her company. I assured her that I would not make use of anything in her journals, but hoped that she was still moving forward with having them printed and bound. I signed the letter, *With regret and humility*, and sent it by certified mail to her house.

It came back two days later, unopened.

One evening around the holidays, when I was feeling especially low, I drove up to Mrs. W—'s house. I couldn't get past the front gate, of course, but I could just make out the grand mansion in the distance, tucked

behind a curve. The grounds were decorated for Christmas, strung with beautiful, festive lights; the house itself was done up too, with potted poinsettias in front of
the door and a grand, living Christmas tree. I knew that
Mrs. W—, like me, was spending the holidays on her
own. The decorations were mostly for the people who
worked there. I felt an intense loneliness and drove back
down the hill, passing several other mansions I'd visited
in the endless procession of luncheons and parties. All
of these places were closed to me now. They always had
been, even when I was in them.

Just a few weeks ago, I was flipping through the *Los Angeles Times* when I came across a picture of Fiona. She looked
the same as she had the last time I saw her—beautiful,
cold—and the radiance of her smile could not disguise,
for me, the essential hardness. The caption announced
that Fiona Morgan, head of the Harrington Foundation
and cochair of the Council of Family Foundations, had
just been named chairperson of the County Art Museum.
Fiona, the woman who claimed to be tired of such commitments. Fiona, who did not care for art. She was pictured with the former chair, the museum director, and
the mayor, at a dinner celebrating her appointment.

Mrs. W— once told me that the most important history never made it into written accounts; that she, and
people like her, *were* history. She was right, of course.
People like her, like the Harringtons, the Bakers, the
Fehringers—they're the ones who make the world run.
The rest of us might see some small result of their
machinations—in decisions made by supposedly inde-

pendent officials; in laws favorable to their interests; in the buildings and institutions that bear their names. But these signs are mere tips of an iceberg whose breadth and influence stay well out of sight. The historians, the researchers, have no idea of how much they miss. They simply can't *see* the Mrs. W—s of the world. To those who might study their influence, they are more than inaccessible. They're as invisible as phantoms, as gods.

There was one other loose end that I wanted to tie up—so last May, about a year after I'd gone to dig around, I drove back up to Cambria. On the morning I left, a bad accident was clogging the 101; my navigation app directed me to stay on the 5, through the Grapevine and into the Central Valley. Per its instructions, I got off near Buttonwillow and headed west. The land there, away from the irrigated fields, was barren as the moon. Even as Los Angeles was bursting with spring flowers, even as the Sierras were still covered with snow, the Central Valley looked like the desert it was. The brown earth was cracked and dry, and swirls of dust moved across the endless flat earth like apparitions risen from the ground. Nothing grew there, nothing broke up the relentless drab, except the falling-down gas stations I passed every forty miles or so, which looked like they'd been forgotten in time.

After a while I started to see shapes on the horizon—trees? No. As I got closer, I realized they were oil pumps—the long-necked, heavy-headed things I'd heard called *nodding donkeys*, stretching north and south as far as I could see. There were hundreds of them, maybe thousands, with their heads bowing up and down: like a field of grazing beasts. As I got closer I saw that many of them were painted bright colors: yellow and pink, lime green and teal blue, mixed in with the gray or black pumps that were common in LA. Maybe this was the oil company's attempt at humor, or at making the scene less bleak. But bleak it was. This field, which stretched for miles, was surrounded by a fence, littered with stacks of pipeline and discarded machines; there was not a person anywhere in sight. I couldn't help but think of the pumps as living things, sucking the oil from deep in the earth. I moved through the nodding creatures, which now surrounded me on either side, with awe and a bit of fear. Finally I pulled over and got out of the car. I covered my nose with my shirt against the dust and fumes, and gazed out at the endless spread of them, listened to the eerie creaking of the pumps. It felt like the apocalypse, or at least the Twilight Zone; it felt like a place beyond man.

And yet fields like this had made the W—s rich. This very field might have been one of Langley's. I thought how strange it was that Mrs. W—'s beautiful Bel Air mansion, her exclusive couture and expensive art, all the fineries of her existence, had been made possible by what happened—was still happening—here. This desolate place, where men's lungs filled with petroleum fumes and their hands were slicked with oil and dust blew into in every sun-cracked wrinkle. Her grandfather had spent much of his life in such places. Mrs. W—'s life was shiny and clean, and this world was so dirty. I had never thought this through until now.

I found Lorena Castillo at the Anchor Café, and my timing was lucky—she had just given notice. She'd been accepted into graduate school at UC San Diego, in environmental studies, and she'd saved up money so she could take three weeks to hike the John Muir Trail before she moved to San Diego. We went back to the Sand Bar and I told her what I'd found—that she was right about the identity of the driver in the accident; that the Larsons were now aware that Charles was not at fault; and that Steven's family was so disgusted they had disowned him. I told her that she was also right in thinking that if she pushed things any further, her brother's family, and her parents, might lose the rest of the hush money. I did not tell her how I had found this all out; I didn't mention Mrs. W— or Fiona. Part of this was shame about my own role, the way I'd let myself be used. But it also felt so futile, so ridiculous. I did not want her to know that her brother's story, his paralyzing injury and the Larsons' deaths, had been reduced to gossip, fodder for machinations of the wealthy. I did not want any of them to suffer that final indignity.

"So that bastard's going to get away with it, isn't he?" she asked.

"Yes, he is," I said.

"And there's nothing I can do to try and hold him accountable—at least, not without risking my family's situation."

"No."

She sat in silence for a moment, staring out at the beach, the seagulls gliding over the sand. Despite this disappointing news, she seemed calmer somehow. The fact that things had happened the way she said they had, this acknowledgment of the truth, appeared to give her some comfort.

"I can't wait to get out of here," she said, taking a

long gulp from her beer. "I can't wait to be away from this and get on with my life." She tucked a strand of wind-loosened hair behind her ear, and I noted again her smooth, unblemished skin, the determined jaw, the burden that seemed to weigh on her shoulders.

"I'm so sorry for what you and your family have had to go through," I said, and meant it.

She turned toward me, and I saw now how tenuous her grip was on her emotions, how hard-fought and fragile her strength. "Thank you," she said, meeting my eyes. "Thank you for giving a shit."

I walked with her out to the parking lot, and as we turned the corner, we saw something on the ground—a dead bird. My stomach lurched. It was in an awful, awkward position, sitting on its rump with its wings half-spread, shoulders hunched, its face to the sky. The body was gray, lined with white stripes, a bit of yellow on its back. I sucked in my breath and averted my eyes, but Lorena said, "Oh," and walked toward it. "He's just a baby. I've got to move him so he doesn't get run over."

I stared off at nothing, contemplating this horrid end to an already bad afternoon.

"He's alive," she said, as she crouched down over him. And this seemed even worse somehow, that we'd come upon this grievously injured bird and would have to watch it die. Gently, Lorena cupped her finger over the tiny, fig-sized thing and lifted him by the shoulders, her other hand sliding under him for support.

"Should I get a box or something?" I asked, feeling useless.

"Yes," she said evenly. She walked over to a low wall that bordered the lot and sat with the bird in her palm.

I dug around in a garbage bin and found a cardboard container the size of a shoe box. When I got back to where Lorena was sitting, the bird was standing up and perched on her finger. Lorena smiled at the surprise on my face.

"I think he was just stunned," she said. "Nothing seems broken. He moved his wings and his neck's okay, and look how tight he's holding on."

The bird's grip was so firm that I could see the indentation on Lorena's finger. He managed to stay upright, a pretty little thing, dazed but in one piece. We sat there, the three of us, the bird's face not more than two feet from my own. Lorena was at ease, and her calmness calmed the hurt creature.

"How did you . . . ?"

She shrugged. "I think he flew into that window there." She nodded toward a plane of glass at the back of the restaurant. "Poor baby. He's still just getting his wings."

The bird considered me dully, and I saw the beauty of his head and wings, the harsh effectiveness of his feet. He seemed content on Lorena's finger. Then he suddenly blinked twice and his eyes grew bright and wide, as if, looking at me, he realized he was staring at a monster. He shrugged his shoulders and then off he flew, as sudden and effortless as if nothing had happened.

Lorena smiled. "We did good."

"*You* did good," I said. And it seemed to me that I was looking at someone who possessed both calm and magic. Every time I've felt especially down these last months, I remember that scene: how Lorena knew what to do in a moment of crisis; how she gathered death and turned it into life.

* * *

I made one other change after I gave up on my dissertation—last fall, I started to exercise again. I'd drive over to Baldwin Hills, through my parents' old neighborhood, up to the calm, expansive park at the top. There, I'd hike or run the trails, past the lake near the entrance, and smile at the middle-aged ladies walking through the Japanese garden, the old men trailing their dogs. I'd make a couple of loops around the park, enjoying the views, before heading back down to the flats.

One day in November, after the first big storm of the season, I drove to the park, made my way to the overlook, and stared back down at the city. The view from Baldwin Hills is my favorite view of Los Angeles. There, you can see the complex lay of the land, the way the plains jut up against the mountains. That day, the downtown buildings gleamed in the afternoon sun, and the mountains were covered with snow. To the left were the Hollywood Hills, sprinkled with houses, stamped with their indelible sign. In those hills, and in others that extended westward to the ocean, the wealthy of the city retreated.

Standing there, gazing over the city, I imagined what it had looked like in Langley W—'s time. By the time my grandfather immigrated from Japan in the early 1920s, the contours of the city were already set—as were the parameters within which he could move. But Langley arrived from New Hampshire in 1898, a workingman, but white, when Los Angeles was still a tiny enclave. None of the neighborhoods I saw below had even been imagined; just a few dirt roads traversed the wide basin; and there were stretches of open fields as far as the eye could see. I wondered if he had looked out at the untouched land and planned to bend it to his desires. I wondered if he knew that he'd be shaping a city. From where I stood, I could see the region's vastness and beauty, the particular West Coast drama of mountains, valley, and sea. And yet a thousand feet away, just across from where I stood, there was a giant oil field: dusty and barren, full of rusted machines, the metal donkeys perpetually nodding.

Despite Professor Rose's encouragement, I never made use of the W—s' history. It wasn't just that I no longer had access to the original source material, or that I was restricted by Mrs. W—'s agreement. There was also my sense, quite simply, that Mrs. W— didn't want their story told. On the one hand, I could not understand this. While other founding families had volumes written about them, the W—s were fading. None of Mrs. W—'s children bore the family name or even lived in the city, and she would be gone soon too. Even the two buildings that Langley had named were just that, buildings; they blended in with the countless other named structures. That Mrs. W— would not want her family's contributions acknowledged was beyond my comprehension. But maybe it is the error of the likes of me—the unrecorded and invisible—to assume that others want to be known. Maybe this desire, which Mrs. W— clearly didn't share, was what had driven me to the study of history.

And maybe Mrs. W— was right. For while other family histories are preserved in public lore, many of those family patriarchs came to sad ends, their careers marred by tragedy and scandal. Edward Doheny, like Langley W—, made his fortune in oil, but was implicated in a government bribery scandal and lost his son to a murder-suicide. William Mulholland brought water to the city—but drained a once-fertile region of the state, and designed a faulty dam whose failure killed hundreds. That was the kind of notoriety the W—s managed to avoid. They'd had no scandals, no real tragedies from Langley's time down—not until Steven, at least. No wonder Mrs. W— wanted no part of publicity. No wonder she'd gone to such lengths to suppress the truth of her son's accident.

If Langley W—'s story remains unknown, his discoveries changed the world. When he was a young hired hand in the Central Valley, he could hardly have imagined that the substance he drew from the earth would alter human dealings, sway elections, spawn endless cycles of war, and change the quality of the air, the contours of the land. So much of modern life, both terrible and good, has risen from the discovery of oil. Even if Langley lacked the proper recognition in history books, his legacy has already been written.

As for me, I've curtailed my ambitions. My life, with its lectures and office hours, its humble, striving students, may be modest—but at least it is mine. If my trips to the Central Coast have reminded me of anything, it is how transient we humans are. Looking up at the hills, or out over the ocean, I know they'll be here longer than I— that the fog will roll in, the waves curl and crash, long after everyone now living is gone. Maybe that's what Steven J— lost sight of as he sped down the airstrip that night—that we are ephemeral, not indestructible. Charles Larson and his son learned this the hard way. They were only here for a moment, despite what their families controlled, and their wealth could not protect them.

Only when I think of Mrs. W— does my equilibrium

break. A year and a half after the last time I saw her, she still haunts my memory and conscience. I spent four months working for her, and had no better understanding of who she was at the end of that time than I did at the beginning. She was a misanthrope who gave generously to causes she claimed to despise; an aesthete who welcomed people who didn't share her sensibilities; a professed hater of the social niceties that she performed with such grace; a harsh mother who bailed out her wayward son at his moment of greatest need, at the cost of another family's peace. One day I'll make sense of how I could have betrayed a woman who, for all of her airs and idiosyncrasies, had been nothing but kind to me. One day I'll understand what my time with her meant, and if that's the most I can do, I will have to be satisfied.

But this, this incomplete chronicle, is the closest I'll get to telling the W—s' story. I can isolate—as I've done here—small snapshots of their lives, incidents and tales that are sifted through with the doings of more public families. I can recognize, as few others can, the W—s' part in the making of Los Angeles. But that's as far as I'll ever go. I have done enough damage already, by allowing Mrs. W—to believe that I had her best interest at heart; by accepting her generosity; by becoming the instrument for uncovering her family's deepest shame. I'm grateful for the experiences I gained with Mrs. W—, but I will not—due to what little is left of my sense of decency—disclose what I learned of her family's past. I won't make use of the journals and letters that the historians so desire. I won't even acknowledge her name.

The End

Acknowledgments

My deepest thanks, as ever, to Kyoko Uchida, Jennifer Gilmore, and Felicia Luna Lemus for their careful readings of this book. And to the whole team at Akashic Books for their tireless work and support—again.

Also available by Nina Revoyr from Akashic Books

LOST CANYON
320 pages, trade paperback, $15.95; hardcover, $26.95

- Finalist for the Southern California Independent Booksellers Association Award (SCIBA) for Adult Fiction
- One of the *San Francisco Chronicle's* 100 Recommended Books of 2015

"Revoyr [is] an edgy and spellbinding writer." —*Booklist* (starred review)

WINGSHOOTERS
248 pages, trade paperback, $15.95

- A *Booklist* Book of the Year
- Finalist for SCIBA's 2011 Fiction Award
- Winner of the 2011 Midwest Booksellers Choice Award
- Winner of the first annual Indie Booksellers Choice Award

THE AGE OF DREAMING
320 pages, trade paperback, $16.95

- Finalist, 2008 *Los Angeles Times* Book Prize
- Top Five Books of 2008, the *Advocate*
- Best Books of 2008, *January* magazine

"Fast-moving, riveting, unpredictable, and profound." —*Library Journal*

SOUTHLAND
348 pages, trade paperback, $15.95

- A *Los Angeles Times* Best Seller
- Winner of a 2004 ALA Stonewall Honor Award in Literature
- Winner of the 2003 Lambda Literary Award
- Nominated for an Edgar Award
- Selected for the *LA Times* Best Books of 2003 List

THE NECESSARY HUNGER
336 pages, trade paperback, $15.95

"*The Necessary Hunger* is the kind of irresistible read you start on the subway at 6 p.m. on the way home from work and keep plowing through until you've turned the last page." —*Time*

"Quietly intimate, vigorously honest, and uniquely American . . . Tough and tender without a single false note." —*Kirkus Reviews*